Blazing Justice

THEA LANDEN

Also by Thea Landen

The Edge of the Sphere
Tangled in His Possession
Train Hard, Rest Harder
Searching the Skies
Defying the Skies
Surrendering the Skies
Chasing the Skies
Conquering the Skies
Sonata for Springtime
The Deeper We Go
A Flame Among the Stars
Disintegration
Disintegration: The Prequels
The Fall of the Midnight Scorpions
Sweet Escape
Hunting Astrid
Andromeda's Tear
Fire Beyond the Frost
Closing Montage
Seductive Suspect
Out of Orbit
Flight of the Dragon Queen
Elysium
Second Skin

Copyright © 2020 Thea Landen
All rights reserved

The characters and events portrayed in this book are fictitious. Any similarity to real persons,
living or dead, is coincidental and not intended by the author.

No part of this book may be reproduced, or stored in a retrieval system, or transmitted in any
form or by any means, electronic, mechanical, photocopying, recording, or otherwise, without express written permission of the publisher.

Enchant & Excite Media, LLC

A Note From the Author

Blazing Justice tells the story of prosecutor Celeste McConnell and her involvement in a high-profile murder case. Along the way, she meets three attractive men who show a romantic interest in her. As the case progresses, it's up to you, the reader, to decide who she shares her "happily ever after" with. Each man has his own alluring qualities and offers a unique relationship, but the choice is yours.

Please do not read this book straight through, in a linear fashion! At the end of each section, two choices will be presented to you. Select your preference and turn to the next part of the plot you choose. Follow your heart, and happy reading!

THE SCENE OF THE CRIME

I pulled my jacket tighter around my shoulders and shivered. A thin sliver of moon illuminated the parking lot, reminding me how much I'd rather be back home, snuggled under a pile of blankets. Work obligations beckoned, however. So much for a nine to five job.

Hurrying across the gravel, I headed toward the cluster of flashing lights and fluorescent tape. The first person I spotted was a familiar one. "Detective Delgado!" I called out.

"Hey there!" A wide grin spread across Alex Delgado's face when I approached the police barrier. He looked me up and down and chuckled. "Nice jeans."

"Yeah, well, you don't get the fancy suit when I get dragged out of bed in the middle of the night."

"Fair enough," he said. "So, what's going on? The DA's office doesn't trust us with this investigation and they sent a babysitter?"

I kicked at the ground with the toe of my sneaker. "This isn't Manhattan. We don't get this level of brutal crime as often out here in the 'burbs." Sighing, I shrugged my shoulders in a half-hearted apology. "You know how Hayes gets. He wants everything done exactly, perfectly right, from protecting the chain of evidence to making sure no one's rights get trampled."

"If he cares so much, maybe he should be out here in the cold."

"I could get behind that idea." I rubbed my hands together, then shoved them deep into my pockets. "Unfortunately, I'm at the bottom of the food chain, so here I am, doing the unglamorous work."

Delgado's chocolate brown eyes twinkled in the darkness. "Well, Miss McConnell, you are a pleasant sight after the night I've had."

"It's one o'clock in the morning. You can drop the formalities and call me Celeste."

He laughed again. "Sure thing, Celeste."

I would have been content making small talk with the genial Detective Delgado indefinitely, but we had a job to do. Another chill rippled through my body as I remembered why I'd been sent out to the Meadowbrook Gardens apartment complex. This time, the unsettled feeling didn't stem from the miserable weather. "How bad is it?" I asked.

The smile disappeared from his face, and he ran his hand through his cropped black hair. "I won't lie to you. It's bad. Probably the worst I've seen."

"Fantastic."

"You sure you want to see this?" His forehead creased with concern. "I won't tell the boss if you hang back and do whatever you have to do from afar."

"No, it's okay," I said. "I'm sure I'll be looking at the crime scene photos for the next couple months, anyway. But thanks."

He nodded. "No problem."

I took a deep breath and let it out, clouding the air in front of me. "Might as well get it over with, then."

Delgado grabbed the yellow tape and lifted it up. With his other hand on the small of my back, he guided me underneath, into the courtyard of Meadowbrook Gardens. Bursts of light from the photographer's camera flashed from beside a row of hedges. I shuffled toward the shrubbery, bracing myself for what I was about to see.

To my dismay, the detective's warning hadn't been an exaggeration. The victim lay in a dark red pool, the viscous fluids seeping into the cracks of the walkway. Blood matted the ends of her hair and drenched her blouse...or what was left of it. Shreds of striped cotton and torn flesh intermingled in disorganized patterns across her chest. A wave of nausea churned in my stomach, and I had to look away.

Delgado touched my arm from behind. "Let's concentrate on the facts."

I nodded, afraid to open my mouth.

"The victim is Sherri Strahan, twenty-seven years old. Moved into the Gardens about eight months ago, according to her neighbors. Obviously, the cause of death appears to be multiple stab wounds."

"Mm-hmm."

He continued with his recitation. "She's got a record, but nothing in this jurisdiction," he said. "Some drug charges, served a couple months here and there, nothing major."

"Do you think it's a deal gone bad?"

"I don't know." He rubbed at his hair again. "As you're aware, the dealers around here aren't strangers to violence. But this level of brutality seems a bit much for the small operations going on in this town."

I risked a glance back at the dead body. "Stabbings are personal, intimate. Or so they say." Sherri's cold eyes stared back at me and I turned around. "Unless we've got a lunatic on our hands, I'd guess she knew her killer."

"Agreed."

A door opened on the opposite side of the courtyard. Four people exited the building: another detective I recognized, two uniformed officers, and a man in the same state of hasty rumpled dress as I was. "Who's that?" I asked.

"Good question," Delgado said. "Let's go find out."

Glad to get away from the gory crime scene, I trailed after him as we made our way across the courtyard. One of the officers opened the rear door of a squad car and the other helped the unknown man inside. He offered no resistance and stared straight ahead as they locked him in.

"Jenkins, what did you find?" Delgado asked.

The other detective nodded a greeting to

me before responding. "That's Nick Lattimer, another relative newcomer in town." He jerked his head toward the squad car. "Turns out he has a bit of history with the vic."

I raised an eyebrow. "Oh?"

"You'll love this, Miss McConnell," Jenkins said, smirking. "While doing some digging on the recently departed, one of our guys learned that she testified against a Jeremy Lattimer after a drug bust last year, sending him away for a long time."

Delgado let out a low whistle. "That can't be a coincidence."

"Probably not. But Mr. Lattimer volunteered to come in for questioning."

"You learned a lot awfully quickly," I said. "Not that I mind if it gets us out of the cold a little faster. But how did you find out about all of this?"

Jenkins gestured toward the block of apartment buildings. "The neighbor who stumbled across the body recognized her and pointed us to her unit." He let out a little cough. "The door was unlocked and there were papers all over her dresser, so we took a brief look around."

"Lucky us." Another icy blast whipped across my exposed face and I winced. "Thank goodness for neighbors in a small town."

I peered into the backseat of the car to get a better look at this Nick Lattimer. Sandy hair fell across his eyes and a day's worth of stubble peppered his cheeks. His hands were buried in the pockets of his hoodie and he jiggled one leg. He didn't look like the type of person who could commit such a vicious act, but then, who did?

"Okay, let's be careful with proper procedure here," I said. "He's not under arrest, so he hasn't been read his rights yet, but I don't want to take any chances. If he even *hints* at wanting a lawyer, the questioning stops, understand? We can't risk getting anything he may tell you thrown out due to a technicality."

Delgado offered me a mock salute. "Yes, ma'am."

Before I could say anything else, a series of high-pitched tones emanated from my pocket.

I pulled out the ringing phone and looked at the display. "It's Hayes. I have to take this," I told them.

"Celeste, I wanted to check in and see how things were going." The deep baritone voice of Colin Hayes, my superior at the DA's office, rumbled through the speakers. "What's the story?"

"Shouldn't you be asleep?"

"Not when I'm stressing over the chaos that's going to greet us tomorrow morning when this hits the news," he said. "Tell you what—why don't you get out of the cold and come give me the full report whenever you're done over there?"

"Are you sure?" I asked. "I don't want to—"

"Like I said, I doubt I'll get much sleep tonight anyway."

I'd been to Colin's house before for a couple of work parties since I joined the DA's office last year, but never this late and never by myself. Some of my female colleagues would be jealous over this invitation if they found out, though I had no intentions of being anything but professional. "I'll be in touch," I said. I ended the call with freezing fingers and dropped the phone back into my jacket.

"Everything okay?" Delgado asked.

"Yeah. I just have to go check in with him whenever we're finished."

He looked out over the courtyard. "We've still got guys canvassing the area, looking for witnesses and documenting anything that seems useful. If you want to peek over their shoulders and make sure they're not disturbing evidence, I won't stop you." His attention returned to the man in the squad car. "I'm going back to the station with Mr. Lattimer. You're welcome to come with us and listen in on the questioning, unless you need to report to Hayes as soon as possible."

To go to the station with the police, turn to Page 87.

OR

To visit Colin and fill him in on the investigation, turn to Page 12.

SECOND CHAIR

"I better go check in with Hayes before he starts blowing up my phone every ten minutes," I said. "But remember what I said before about Lattimer's rights. I'm trusting you."

Delgado flashed his charming grin at me again. "I won't let you down."

I got back into my car and cranked up the heat. My fingers started to warm up as I turned the wheel and drove out of the parking lot. Colin Hayes lived in a quiet neighborhood on the outskirts of town. I hadn't been there since his Fourth of July barbecue, but I was reasonably sure I could find it, even in the dark. Within ten minutes, I pulled into his driveway and forced myself back into the cold for the walk up to his front door.

He greeted me wearing nothing but a short-sleeved undershirt and plaid boxer shorts. I tried not to notice the way the thin white cotton clung to the lean muscles of his chest as he ushered me inside. "Come in, come in," he said, shutting the door behind me. "Can I get you anything? Coffee? Tea? Bourbon?"

I shrugged off my jacket. "No, thanks."

We sat in his living room by the fireplace, him sprawled out on the sofa and me perched on an overstuffed armchair. I filled him in on everything that had transpired at the crime scene. "The police have already brought someone in for questioning," I said. "Nick Lattimer lives at Meadowbrook Gardens and his brother's serving time thanks to the victim."

"Interesting." Colin tapped his index fingers together in front of his chin. The dancing flames in the fireplace illuminated the silver streaks threading through his hair. "It's a good lead. Great, even, but we shouldn't jump to any conclusions."

"Of course not," I said. "Our detectives will have a better idea of where we're headed soon."

"They're good guys. I'm sure they will." He stood up and stretched his back, yawning. "With any luck, we'll be getting a warrant for someone before we know it."

Colin walked me back to the front door. He stood close to me, his dark gray eyes staring into mine. "Thank you for taking the time to come over here, Celeste," he said. "It's good to know I can count on you."

I nodded. "You're welcome."

"I like seeing the people in my office so dedicated to their work." He opened the door and a gust of cold air slammed into me. "Now go home and try to get some sleep. I have a feeling we're going to have a busy day tomorrow."

I said my farewells and hurried back to my car. Despite the frigid temperature outside, my cheeks felt flushed as I wondered whether I'd be able to get through the next day without imagining what color boxers Colin wore under his suits.

***

"Son of a bitch!"

I jerked my head away from my computer screen, as did my two officemates. Colin's angry shout echoed down the hallway and I could hear footsteps thudding on the linoleum. "Uh-oh," said Daniel the clerk. "Someone's not happy."

Angie, who sat at the desk adjacent to mine, rolled her eyes while I wheeled my chair back. "I'll see what's going on," I told them. Tentatively, I stood up and peeked my head out into the corridor.

Colin stormed toward me and slowed when he reached my door. Anger darkened his face and tightened in his neck. "What happened?" I asked, trying to keep my voice soft and neutral.

"Lattimer made bail. I don't know what the judge was thinking." He started moving again, though he paced in tight circles in front of me. "That's what I get for sending that imbecile Benson to do the arraignment hearing."

I frowned. "How much was it?"

"Does it matter? Lattimer's back out on the streets, which I'm sure will make the public think *so* highly of this office. I can just see tomorrow's newspaper headlines now." His jaw clenched, his rage still simmering within. "He had a motive to kill her, and a knife covered in the victim's blood was found in his garbage can. For crying out loud, she was all but murdered right on his doorstep!"

"I know, I know." I debated whether to try and calm him down or stay out of his way. "Judges make mistakes. We'll find a way to make this okay."

Colin finally stopped in one place and his face began to lighten to a lesser shade of crimson. "You're right," he said, letting out a long breath. "We *will* win this case. You and I."

My right eyebrow shot up. "What?"

"From now on, I want you assisting me in everything involving this murder. I don't care how long you've been here. I know I can trust you."

Flustered, I didn't know how to respond. "But I...I mean, shouldn't you—"

"I've made my decision." His fury had subsided, and the calm, confident prosecutor with a knack for winning over juries stood before me once more. "It was my fault for not giving you this assignment earlier, especially since you were on-scene at the very beginning."

"I...I'm flattered you think so highly of me."

"Lattimer and his attorney are coming in at the end of the week to discuss a plea deal. Finish up whatever you're working on and come see me after lunch so we can start preparing." He placed his hand on my shoulder and fixed me in his intense gaze. "This could be a big break for you. Let's find a way to nail this guy."

I was sure my face was as red as Colin's had been when I stepped back inside the office, albeit for a different reason. "Ooh, look at you," Daniel said. "Someone's the new favorite around here."

Angie batted her eyelashes at me. "I trust you, Celeste. Let's go win this case together!" she said in a tone clearly intended to mock the conversation they'd overheard.

"Oh, stop it." I should have been annoyed with their teasing, but I still laughed.

She exhaled loudly and shook her head. "I'd kill to be in your shoes. I wish he paid that kind of attention to me."

"He's not paying special attention to me. He's focused on the case."

"Uh-huh, sure," Daniel said. "And as he pointed out, you've been part of the case since the beginning."

I couldn't resist goading them on a little bit. "True. And I don't think I ever told you what he was wearing when I dropped by on the night of the murder. Or, rather, what he *wasn't* wearing."

"You've been holding out on us!" Angie wadded up a piece of scrap paper and chucked it at me. "Colin is, like, the most eligible bachelor in the county. If you saw him practically naked, I need all the details!"

"I'm sorry to disappoint you, then." I plopped back into my desk chair. "You two can laugh and gossip all you want, but I don't know what you think is going to happen."

"We're just joking around with you," Daniel said.

"Mm-hmm." The clock on my computer indicated I had an hour before lunch and I wanted to try to complete the file I had open. "Look, everything between Colin and me has always been strictly professional. I like having this job, so I intend to keep it that way."

Angie let out another melodramatic sigh. "Fine. You're no fun."

I ate lunch at my desk in order to finish up some work before finding Colin. Our first order of business was to schedule an appointment with Lattimer's attorney to discuss a plea. On the morning of the meeting,

I put my coat and my purse in my office as soon as I arrived, and then headed for the conference room.

The door to the men's room opened as I walked down the hallway. To my surprise, I came face-to-face with Nick Lattimer. "Excuse me," I mumbled.

Recognition lit up his eyes. "You..." he said. "You were there...that night."

"Mr. Lattimer, you really shouldn't be talking to me without your attorney present."

I tried to move around him and he blocked my path. "No, listen. I didn't do this! I didn't kill her!"

"Mr. Lattimer, I—"

"You saw me that night, you saw how I volunteered to go down to the station. I didn't argue, I didn't resist, and I didn't even want a lawyer with me. I thought I was helping!" His lips curved down and, for a moment, I wondered if he was going to burst into tears right there in the middle of the hallway. "I don't know how this happened. You have to believe me."

The expression of weariness on his face and the notes of desperation in his voice tugged at my sympathies. However, we sat on opposite sides of the table in this matter. "Mr. Lattimer, please. I can't have this conversation with you." When he opened his mouth to speak again, I put up a hand to stop him. "I believe we're both due in the conference room right now. Your attorney will plead your case there."

He didn't try to stop me again when I continued down the corridor. I quickly slipped into the conference room, not caring if he was behind me or not. Colin and the other attorney were already inside, and we exchanged perfunctory greetings. I set my pile of paperwork on the table and sat down in the chair Colin pulled out for me.

Nick joined us a moment later. "This might be a waste of time," Miles, his lawyer, said. "My client is still insisting he didn't do it."

"Don't they all?" Colin shot back.

"Make your offer and we'll think about it."

"No, we won't!" Nick shouted. "This is

insane! This is—"

"Nick." Miles patted his shoulder. "We have to at least listen to what they have to say."

Colin outlined the terms of our proposed plea bargain. Across from me, Nick glowered silently and I took care not to meet his gaze. Most lawbreakers who came through our office eventually took a deal; then again, this was the most serious crime we'd dealt with since I joined the DA's office in this quiet jurisdiction. With my limited experience, I wasn't sure how accused murderers were supposed to act.

Miles and his client stood up. "Thanks for going through the motions with us. I'll call you tomorrow."

He moved toward the door, but Nick stayed in place. "I didn't kill Sherri," he said, his voice even and quiet. I stiffened in my chair when he stared straight at me. "I don't care what you think your evidence says. It's wrong."

"Nick, come on."

They finally left, and I let out the breath I'd been holding. Colin closed his file folder and dropped it on top of the stack. "Well, I'll be glad when we put him away for good," he said.

I didn't answer. Recalling my encounter with Nick plagued me for the rest of the day. The vehemence with which he claimed his innocence couldn't be denied. If it turned out he played no role in the victim's murder, then I'd feel terrible not only about his ordeal but the failings of the justice system as a whole. On the other hand, his demeanor in the conference room was unnerving. Had I looked into the eyes of a cold-blooded killer?

Before I left to go home, I wandered by Colin's office. He sat inside at his desk, his head propped up on one hand as he stared at his computer. I stood in the doorway and cleared my throat. "Got a minute?" I asked.

He leaned back in his seat. "For you? Of course."

I knotted my fingers in front of me and chewed on my bottom lip. "I've been thinking about our meeting with Lattimer and his attorney," I said. "And whether or not he's guilty."

"Ah." With his rolled-up sleeves and loosened tie, Colin almost appeared relaxed, yet I knew the pit bull of a prosecutor always lurked within. "Why the sudden doubts?"

I debated whether or not to tell him about my encounter with Nick in the hallway. Honesty won out in this atmosphere of justice. "He talked to me privately outside before we all sat down. Even though I told him not to."

"I see."

"And the way he...I don't know."

Colin rested his foot on his knee and rocked back and forth in his chair. "Let me guess. He told you he didn't do it?"

"Well, yes."

A small smile twisted up one side of his mouth. "Did you expect him to say otherwise?"

"I guess not."

"If every case were clear cut, we'd be out of a job," he said. "Plenty of juries have convicted on less than what we've got."

I cared more about his personal opinion than legal precedent. "Do you think he killed her?"

The chair stopped bouncing. He stroked his chin, as if giving my question serious consideration. "I think that based on the evidence available to us, there is a very, very high chance he did, and I've yet to see something proving otherwise," he finally said. "And I know you won't find that very reassuring right now, but it's the best I can offer in this imperfect business of ours."

I managed a little chuckle. "It helps. Somewhat."

The amused expression remained on Colin's face as he watched me. "I won't lie, this job is difficult some days. It can eat away at you if you're not careful."

"So I've been told."

"But you're a good attorney, Celeste. I saw that from the start with you. Be true to the law and true to yourself, and I'm certain you'll go far in this field."

I nodded, hoping the blush rising up my neck into my cheeks wasn't noticeable. "Thanks, Colin." Turning around, I left to collect my things so I could go home. With luck, I thought, I'd feel better about the case in the morning.

To trust in Colin's beliefs regarding the case, turn to Page 27.

OR

To share concerns and doubts with Detective Delgado, turn to Page 51.

LATE NIGHTS AND LEGAL BRIEFS

I tried to push aside any thoughts regarding Nick Lattimer and who he may or may not have killed for the rest of the night. Sleep came more easily than I expected and I woke up the following day feeling refreshed. Colin was right, I decided. Nick had been questioned, arrested, and indicted all according to the law, and I had to trust in our judicial system.

In the morning, I stopped by his office again on the way to my desk. The polished professional had returned, ready for a new day of work with his jacket and tie perfectly in place. I knocked on the open door and he looked up at me with his clear gray eyes. "Good morning," he said. "Feeling any better today?"

"I am." I fidgeted with my purse and tried not to squirm under his probing stare. "Thanks for yesterday's pep talk."

Colin stood up and crossed the room. "You would have reached the same conclusions on your own." He closed the gap between us, coming so close I could smell his aftershave. "I meant what I said about noticing your aptitude from your very first interview here. I do hope you plan on staying for some time, as I look forward to seeing what you could accomplish in this office."

The temperature of the room suddenly felt like it had climbed ten degrees. I attempted to subtly unbutton my coat to get some air as I inched backward and prayed I wasn't turning a flaming shade of red. "I...I should go check my e-mail."

He's your superior, he's a professional, he's only interested in you as a colleague.... I tried to convince myself Colin's primary concern was the quality of my work as I made my escape and hurried to my desk. Luckily, my officemates had yet to arrive and I could regain my composure in private. My caseload demanded attention and I needed to focus on my priorities.

Months passed, the time flying by as we were caught up in the whirlwind of preparing for trial. Motions had to be filed, a jury had to be selected, and the mountains of paperwork only grew. There were weeks when I felt as if I spent more time at the office with Colin than in my own apartment, which Angie loved to tease me about. Throughout the entire process, I tried to maintain a friendly, yet appropriate working relationship with the handsome man who wielded such a commanding presence, even if my mind had a tendency to wander during our late nights.

We took over one of the conference rooms

with our multitude of boxes and folders. Less than a week before the beginning of the trial, I stood in there and tried not to become overwhelmed. *Deep breaths*, I reminded myself as I thought about how this case was the most newsworthy event the town had seen in a long time. Though I tried to appear confident, I worried about being dragged too close to the center of the storm.

Colin joined me, nudging a box away from the doorway with his foot. "Let's finalize the order of our witness list," he said. "We might as well get that out of the way before we start organizing the exhibits."

We got to work, ignoring the departures of our colleagues and the darkening sky outside the window. I fetched a container of yogurt from the breakroom refrigerator and scarfed it down as a quick dinner. "It looks like we even outlasted the cleaning crews tonight," I joked when I returned.

He glanced up from the file in his hands. "You can go home if you'd like," he said. "I'm just trying to stay on top of everything so I don't feel rushed at the last minute."

"No, it's fine. If you're here, I should be, too." I looked down at my feet and winced. "Though if you don't mind, I think I need to lose the high heels for the day."

I stepped out of my shoes, shrinking two and a half inches, and kicked them under the table. Colin laughed and unknotted his loosened tie, tossing it over one of the chairs. "Anything else you need to get comfortable?"

"I think I'm okay."

"Are you sure?"

I contemplated the question. "Give me one minute."

Slipping back out into the hallway, I looked up and down the corridor to make sure no one else was around. I reached up underneath my skirt and hooked my thumbs into the waistband of my pantyhose. When they slid off my hips and down my legs, I breathed a sigh of relief.

Back inside, I tucked the discarded stockings into one of my shoes. Colin looked me up and down, and a smile crept over his lips. "Better?" he asked.

"Much."

I rejoined him at one side of the table to survey our clutter. Almost every square inch of the surface was covered. "I set aside the police reports we're using," he said. "Next up is the medical examiner's report."

I rummaged through the stack where I thought I'd last seen the document. "Here," I said, passing the packet over.

"No, not this one. There's a highlighted copy somewhere."

"Oh, right. I think it's in the pile we were going through earlier."

I reached over to the other side of the table, brushing across the front of Colin's body. He shifted to let me pass, which only resulted in trapping me between him and the heavy furniture. Startled by the realization of his close proximity and the warmth pressing against me, I froze in place.

His hand rested on my waist. My heart raced and I steadied myself with one palm on the table. The scorching imprint of his touch felt like it was going to burn a hole through my blouse. *Is this really happening?*

I dared to swivel my head to the side. Steel gray eyes met my gaze, hunger simmering within them. He moved closer and my breath caught in my throat.

Soft lips captured my mouth in a tender kiss. Surprised, I dropped the papers I'd been holding. His grip on me tightened as the gentle gesture became a more forceful exploration. I let his tongue probe into mine, and a rush of heat flooded through me.

When I tried to turn toward him, I found I still couldn't move. He pulled his mouth away, but didn't step back to allow me to escape his grasp. Though unable to deny the exhilarating thrill of our illicit kiss, I was anxious about the possible consequences. "Are you sure we...I mean, I don't know if...I can't..." I whispered, glancing away.

Colin steered my face back with a finger on my chin. "Tell me to stop, Celeste, and I will." His deep voice rumbled through his chest, reverberating against my skin. "Just know how long I've been dreaming about touching you like this."

I tried to think through the tempest churning through my mind and body, but my heightened senses pulled me deeper into the lusty storm. His confession echoed in my ears, his musky cologne wafted toward my nose, and the remnants of our kiss lingered on my tongue. The potential dangers lost out to my desires. I needed more.

I circled my hand around the back of his head and drew his lips closer to mine. His tongue plunged inside my mouth and his arms enveloped me from behind. I wanted to touch him, return his embrace, but he still had me pinned against the table. His power over me was intoxicating, and I felt a tremble in my knees.

Colin abandoned my mouth to kiss a trail to my neck. With one hand, he swept aside my hair and brought his lips to my earlobe. "You really are an exquisite woman," he murmured. Steamy breath feathered over my delicate nerves and I shuddered. "Since the day you walked into this office, all eyes have been upon you."

As he spoke, his hands roamed up and down my sides, from the coarse fabric of my skirt to the cream-colored silk of my blouse. His firm caresses across my torso both lulled me into a state of tranquility and further kindled my arousal. "I don't believe you," I said, leaning my head back against his shoulder. "*You're* the one everybody always talks about around here."

His lips skated over the outer ridge of my ear and he chuckled. "I won't lie, I've heard the gossip and the giggling," he said. One thumb grazed the underside of my breasts, while the fingers of his other hand traced a line along my waistband. "But I only care about what you think."

The hem of my blouse slid out of the top of my skirt. Anticipation coiled in my muscles and I struggled for air. "Me?" I managed to squeak out.

"Mm-hmm." His hands slipped beneath my blouse, skin meeting heated skin. "How do you feel about me?"

I squirmed underneath his provocative touch. When my hips rolled back, they met the bulge of his rock-hard erection. Lascivious thoughts consumed me. "I've been thinking about you, too."

"Just thinking about me?" he prodded.

I should have known there was no escaping this line of questioning. "I...I want you."

That wicked laugh resonated in my ear again. "Good." Colin's palms skimmed over my stomach and rose to cup my breasts. He kneaded my flesh through the lacy material and resumed kissing my neck. "A brilliant mind and a killer body," he said as his hands manipulated me. "As soon as I saw you, I knew I had to have you. And you know I am a man who hates to lose."

Deft fingers punctuated his statement by teasing at my stiffened nipples. The resulting sensations sent a jolt of electricity shooting through my body. He held me tight, not permitting me to move and seek out more of his touch. I braced myself on the table and choked back my first moan.

He resumed his broad strokes over my skin, each one dipping a little lower. I tensed when he neared the top of my skirt again, and he laughed. Sharp teeth nipped at my earlobe while his fingers danced along the band of skin below my navel. Every part of me felt as if it was on fire, and I was sure he could sense the heat emanating from between my legs.

Inch by inch, his hand crept toward my dampened panties. He toyed with the triangle of lace and my thighs quivered. A single finger dragged over the length of my cleft, rubbing at the sodden fabric separating me from bliss. I didn't know how much more of this torment I could handle. "Colin," I said, trying to keep the longing out of my voice. "Please."

He withdrew his hand, only to snake it past the elastic waistband. Gliding through the moisture, he drove his finger into my pussy. Pleasure washed over me and my knees weakened. He supported me with one strong arm while sliding a second finger inside me.

In and out he thrust, setting a steady,

deliberate tempo. My hips sought him out, trying to match his rhythm, yet he held me firmly in place. I had no choice but to succumb to his control.

His thumb brushed against my clit and a moan escaped my throat. My fingertips dug into the solid mahogany table as he applied pressure to the bundle of nerves. The first twinges of ecstasy prickled along my skin, desperate to be released. *How long has it been since I last indulged myself?* The questions lingered somewhere in the back of my clouded mind. *How many nights did I tell myself this could never happen?*

His mouth pinpointed every sensitive spot on my neck and collarbone with astonishing accuracy, alternating rough bites with gentle kisses. The combination added to the fire sizzling in my veins and my breaths came in ragged gasps. When he curled his fingers inside me, I cried out and pitched forward.

Colin held me upright as I seized around him. My orgasm wracked my body, sending wave after climactic wave pulsing through me.

I leaned back into his sturdy chest and exhaled, savoring the strength and comfort of his arms.

At long last, he freed me and allowed me to turn around and face him. I gazed into his captivating gray eyes, my lips parted and chest still heaving. "I always knew we could do amazing things together," he said. His finger traced around the neckline of my blouse, tugging at the first button. "That was just the beginning."

Since I'd started working at the DA's office, I'd devoted myself to my caseload, leaving little time for anything outside of my job. Colin awakened feelings in me I hadn't experienced in ages. I craved more, and I was afraid to let him go for even a second.

Heat radiated through his crisp cotton shirt as I ran my hands up his chest. Gripping his shoulders, I tilted my head up and pressed my lips against his. Any semblance of gentleness that had accompanied our first kiss vanished when our tongues met again. They tangled together in a fervent dance, whisking the air from my lungs.

He threaded his fingers through my hair as I leaned back against the table. My hands drifted down to his waist and I pulled him close. His rigid cock swelled through the fabric of his pants, sending another flurry of arousal pooling between my legs. I ached for him.

Sliding back onto the table, I collided with one of the many stacks of papers and folders. "Wait...wait a minute," Colin murmured, breathing heavily.

Waiting seemed like an impossibility. I tugged at his collar in an effort to get him to resume our kiss, but he stepped away and shook his head. "Not here," he said. "I don't want to destroy all our hard work on these files."

I couldn't stifle my laugh. He did have a point, and it was our devotion to our job that drew us to each other. "Very well," I said, hopping down. "What did you have in mind?"

He fixed me in his predatory stare and I swallowed, trying not to shiver beneath its intensity. Grabbing my hand, he led me out to the corridor. "This way."

Colin half-escorted, half-dragged me down the hall, his fingers clenched around mine. Once inside his office, he slammed the door and pinned me against it, resuming his assault on my mouth. My fingers fumbled with the top button of his shirt. Frustrated and unable to think clearly, I abandoned the closures and settled for yanking the bottom of his shirt out of his waistband.

His well-muscled back felt divine beneath my fingertips as I slid my hands inside his clothing. He groaned and pushed against me even harder. "Damn, Celeste," he said, his voice a throaty growl. "It's a wonder I haven't ripped all your clothes off yet."

I responded by giving his lower lip a sharp nibble and groping at his belt buckle. He slithered out of my grasp. "Not yet."

Colin wheeled his chair out from his desk and sat down. When I moved toward him, he put a hand up to stop me. "Strip," he ordered. "Slowly."

I stepped away from the door and stood in front of him. Though sure my cheeks were a vivid shade of scarlet, I unfastened the buttons of my blouse one by one. The silk garment dropped to the floor, pooling at my feet in a shimmering puddle. Next, I dragged down the zipper of my skirt, the long scratch echoing in the room. I let go and it joined the growing pile.

His ravenous stare burned into me and a small smile of approval played upon his lips. So many times he had exerted his command over those before him in the courtroom, bending them to his will. I was the next in line to surrender to his authority...and I loved every second of it.

I reached behind my back to unhook my bra and cast it aside. Free and unrestrained, my breasts jiggled slightly as I struggled to breathe evenly and contain my excitement. Colin nodded and lifted his hand to make a twirling gesture with one finger. I followed the unspoken instruction and turned around. With coy deliberation, I pushed my panties over the swell of my hips and down my legs.

Another choked groan emanated from his

direction. I glanced back at him over my shoulder and saw him stroke his cock through his pants. "Well?" I said, my eyelashes fluttering. "What about you?"

He chuckled. "Your sense of fairness is much appreciated, especially in this office." Standing, he beckoned me toward his desk. Within moments, he cleared an empty spot for me and lifted me onto it.

My mouth watered as I watched him mirror my previous actions. His work shirt cascaded to the floor, revealing his snug white undershirt. Just as it had that night I'd visited him at home, the thin cotton clung to the contours of his chest. I didn't have long to take in the view before he pulled the undershirt off over his head. Dark curls peppered his firm pecs, leading into a trail down the center of his torso.

Before removing his pants, Colin fished his wallet out of his pocket. Offering me a little shrug, he took out a wrapped condom and tossed it onto the desk, where it landed beside me. My pulse pounded in my ears, and I was torn between enjoying the building tension and wanting him inside me again.

He stepped out of his shoes and kicked them aside. His belt followed suit, and then his pants at long last. Clad only in his striped boxer shorts, he came closer to me. It took every ounce of willpower I had not to reach out and tear the underwear off him.

Flashing me that devilish grin, he finally shed the last of his clothing, granting me an unobstructed view of his erection. He took my hand and wrapped it around his cock. "So many nights..." he said, his voice low. "So many nights I fantasized about this exact scenario."

I gave his shaft a squeeze, taking in its impressive girth. As I circled my fingers around him, he retrieved the condom. I let go of his cock so he could sheath its full length and leaned back on my palms.

He nudged my knees apart and stood between them. "Are you sure this is what you want?"

Lust seared through my bloodstream. "Yes," I said, trying to keep the longing out of my answer.

"I don't know...." He trailed a finger down the front of my body, from between my breasts down to the patch of neat curls at my mound. Using the lightest of touches, he teased at the outer edge of my pussy. My spread thighs trembled, and he withdrew his hand. "I don't think you've stated your case strongly enough."

I gritted my teeth together at his taunting. Every nerve in my body yearned for his touch, threatening to drive me insane. "*Please*, Colin."

"Please what?"

He did always win, no matter the game. "Please fuck me," I whispered.

The tip of his erection rubbed along my dampened cleft. He ducked his head down to swipe his lips across mine. "For you, anything," he said.

With one swift movement, he plunged into me, stretching me with his steely cock. I gasped, then moaned as the sensation of being *full* spread throughout my body. My legs clenched around him and I braced myself for his next thrust.

Colin pumped in and out of my cunt with vigor, his fingertips digging into the flesh of my hips. Between the unyielding desk beneath me and his powerful cock, I was trapped once again, unable to escape him as he coaxed pleasure from me. Every time our bodies collided, another crackle of electricity ricocheted through my core.

I clung to his shoulders as he pounded into me. His muscles coiled and tensed, and his breath came in ragged pants. At the mercy of his unrelenting force, I felt the embers of another blazing orgasm begin to ignite and bloom. I closed my eyes and waited to succumb.

He thrust into me so hard I swore we would break the furniture. A raw, primal grunt emitted from his throat and he held me tight. The final impact sent me careening over the precipice into orgasm. Encased in his arms, I let the tremors of my climax overtake me as I gasped for air. Following the frenetic explosion of ecstasy, a delirious buzz settled over me. Eyes still closed, I nestled my cheek against Colin's shoulder, breathing in his musky scent.

He stroked my hair and kissed my temple. "Incredible, Celeste," he murmured. "I do look forward to becoming intimately acquainted with every inch of your body in the future."

I raised my head to meet his gaze. "I don't want this to be a one-time thing either," I confessed.

Smiling, he traced the contour of my cheek with his thumb. "Next time we'll do it right," he said, his chest shaking as he chuckled. "Candlelit dinners, good wine, and making a mess out of my bed."

"I thought we did things pretty well the first time." I joined in his laughter. "But you do paint a very appealing picture."

He helped me off the desk. While he cleaned up, I gathered our clothing and piled it onto his chair. "I'm looking forward to getting to know you better outside the office," I said, slipping my panties back on. "However, we still have a lot of work to do for this trial."

A wide grin spread across Colin's lips before he swept me into his arms for another kiss. "A woman after my own heart."

***

Colin stirred in the chair beside me, stretching his arms over his head as he yawned. He rubbed his eyes and rolled over to face me. "How long was I out?"

I placed a bookmark inside my paperback and shrugged. "Not too long. Twenty minutes, thirty, tops."

"A person could get used to this." He stood and twisted from side to side. Lean muscles rippled beneath his bare skin, and I peered over the top of my sunglasses to better enjoy the view. "I'm going to jump in the water for a bit," he said. "Care to join me?"

"Maybe after I finish this chapter."

I watched him cross the sand to the dazzling turquoise waters of the Caribbean. The trial was over, and we'd achieved our ultimate goal: the jury convicted Nick Lattimer of murder in the second degree. We knew the appeals process could drag on for ages, but

Colin insisted we deserved a reward regardless. When he suggested a week in Aruba, I found it impossible to argue with the skilled attorney yet again.

A gentle breeze drifted through the palm trees, caressing my skin. A vacation was exactly what we'd needed. Despite his reassurances, I'd had some initial qualms about openly dating someone at the office, especially someone in a senior position. Thanks to all my work on the trial, a promotion was in the works for me as well, which didn't help the whispered gossip.

Even a year prior, my younger, less experienced self might have let the petty comments stand in the way of a good thing. With my successes in the legal field, however, came a boost of confidence, and I took it all in stride. I was secure both in who I was as a person and in my relationship with Colin. Building upon our mutual attraction felt natural and wonderful and *right*.

In the distance, Colin's head bobbed in the waves. I placed my book and sunglasses inside my bag and stepped out of the shade. The sun blazed overhead, causing beads of sweat to dot my skin. I yelped when my feet hit the white-hot sand and hurried over to the surf.

He swam toward me and stood in the shallow water. Rivulets trickled over his shoulders and down his chest, and he grinned at me. I returned the smile and waded in up to my ankles.

Standing before the wide-open sea, blissfully happy with the events that had led me to this moment with an amazing man waiting for me, I felt empowered. We'd put a dangerous man in prison, where he could no longer cause harm to others. We'd worked within the structures of our justice system, following the rules and playing fair, and the jury had come to the correct decision with our guidance. Throughout the whole process, we'd discovered an even greater force, and we used our love as motivation, not a distraction, to protect the world from violent criminals.

Together, we'd be unstoppable.

COZY CUPS OF COFFEE

Thoughts of Nick Lattimer's guilt or innocence kept me awake all night. I wanted so badly to be certain about whether or not he'd killed Sherri Strahan, but niggling doubts kept whispering in my ear. The idea of another sleepless night didn't sound appealing, so I decided to seek out another opinion.

I took an early lunch and drove over to the

police station. The clerk at the front desk greeted me by name and I smiled at him. "Is Detective Delgado around, by any chance?" I asked.

"He came in this morning and I haven't seen him leave." The clerk nodded to the door behind him. "You can go right in."

I wandered through the precinct, weaving my way through the scattered desks until I found the man I'd sought. As I approached, Delgado looked up from a stack of folders. His eyes lit up and a wide grin spread across his face. "Miss McConnell!" he said. "What a pleasant surprise!"

Now that I stood in front of him, I felt slightly ridiculous. After all, in doubting my own beliefs, I was also questioning the police work that had led up to Lattimer's arrest. Better to not make an enemy out of the entire department, I reasoned. "Is there somewhere we can talk privately?" I asked, fiddling with the strap of my purse.

"Sure thing."

Delgado stood up and led me into an

empty interrogation room. He closed the door behind us and leaned against the rickety table. "So, what's on your mind, Counselor?"

I sighed. "It's the Lattimer case. This is going to sound crazy, but I...I just don't know if he really did it."

"Okay."

"It's not that I think there was anything wrong with your investigation, or you missed something," I said hurriedly. "But I can't help but think there's a chance he didn't kill that woman."

Delgado stroked his chin. "We followed every single lead we had."

The words came out slowly. I held my breath as a cloud of silence hung over us.

"Though anything's possible, as I'm sure we both know," he said at last.

I exhaled with relief. "I was worried you wouldn't believe me."

"I didn't peg you as the type to try to tank her office's case just for fun." He flashed me his winning smile again, and I felt the tension ease out of my body. "If you think there's something we all missed, it might be worth a second look."

"Are you sure?" I said. "I know you must be busy with other cases, and I don't want to waste your time, and—"

Delgado stood up and tapped my left shoulder, right above my heart. "We're trained to follow our instincts here, our gut feelings," he said, his face close to mine. "I'd never want you to doubt yourself."

The brush of his fingertips felt as if they burned a hole through my blouse. I swallowed and nodded. "Thanks, Detective. I needed to hear that."

My hand was on the doorknob and I was almost out of the room when he spoke again. "Counselor?"

I turned around, certain my skin was bright pink. "Yes?"

He ran his hand through his hair and glanced to the side. "I don't suppose you'd like to grab a cup of coffee with me sometime? Like, a real cup of coffee, not the instant crap we have here at the station."

The flush in my cheeks intensified. "High-quality coffee sounds amazing. I'd love to."

"Give me some time to do more digging on the Lattimer case. How about we meet Thursday morning at eight at that little café by the park?"

"Sounds great!"

I returned to my office and tried to concentrate on my workload, but my thoughts drifted to topics other than motions and murderers. Was it too much to hope for that Delgado also had more on his mind besides the investigation? He'd always been friendly toward me, but he must act that way with everyone, I told myself. *Don't overthink a simple cup of coffee.*

The hours dragged at a painstakingly slow pace until Thursday finally rolled around. I arrived at the coffee shop and chose a table by the window overlooking the park. The sun peeked through the clouds outside, glinting off the surface of the blue-gray waters of a nearby pond. Spring was around the corner, but the weather was chilly enough to make me grateful for the hot beverage in my hands, especially one that tasted so much better than anything I could find at work.

Delgado arrived within a few minutes. He ordered his coffee, then sat across from me, placing a manila folder on the table. Grinning, he slid it over to me.

"What's this?" I asked.

"Could be something, could be nothing." He sipped from his mug. "I'll let you take a look, but only on one condition."

I raised one eyebrow and stared at him through the steam coming off my latte. "Oh? Now you're the one bargaining and making deals?" I teased.

Delgado chuckled. "I promise I'm not trying to steal your job from you."

"Good. I'll hear your terms."

Dark eyes sparkled at me from across the table. "We can spend five minutes discussing the contents of that folder, but then I don't want to talk about work for the rest of the time we're here together."

"I like the way you think." Setting down the

cup, I lifted the cover and skimmed the first page. "Phone records?" I said.

"Yup." He tapped the sheet of paper. "In the days before her death, Sherri Strahan had received a number of calls from an untraceable cell phone. It's hard to track these burner cells, and we'd already arrested Lattimer, so we didn't give it a lot of consideration."

"But...?"

"When you ever so sweetly asked me to go over the file again, I followed up on it. The same number's come up in a couple cases down in the city, all related to a high-powered drug operation." Delgado took another sip and shrugged his shoulders. "Like I said, it might not mean anything. For all we know, it's Lattimer's number anyway, and he's involved in a lot more than he's been letting on, particularly now that his brother's out of commission."

"I'll see what else we can find," I said. "I'll take this to Hayes and we'll talk to our esteemed colleagues down there. Can I keep this copy?"

He winked at me. "Of course. I made it just for you."

"You're too kind." I closed the folder and slipped it into my bag. "But really, Detective, this is great work. I appreciate you listening to my concerns and taking time to review the case at this late stage."

"Don't worry about it." He shook his head and waved his hand. "And since we're not discussing work anymore, enough of that 'Detective' business. Until I'm back at the station, I'd rather be Alex."

"Whatever you'd like, *Alex*."

His smile widened. "So, tell me, Celeste, what do you do when you're not hunting down murderers and locking up criminals?"

"You mean drowning in paperwork and arranging plea bargains that won't make the public hate us?"

"I thought we were too young to be so disillusioned with our jobs already," he said, laughing.

"Maybe." I drank from my mug. "As a fellow public servant, I'm sure you know how our jobs don't leave us with a lot of free time. Some days I feel like I do nothing outside the office except for eating and sleeping."

Alex's mouth curved down in a frown. "Too bad. I'm a little disappointed."

"Why?"

"After we finished this cup of coffee, I was hoping to convince you to see me again outside of our respective work environments." His voice sounded forlorn, yet a spark of mischief flickered in his deep brown eyes. "But I understand if you're too busy...."

I blushed and bit my lower lip. "I think I could manage to make some time for you, Detec—Alex."

"Wonderful." He reached over the table and rested his fingers on my wrist. "And this time, I say we declare a total ban on any conversation related to this case."

A giggle escaped my lips. "You do propose some irresistible deals."

He didn't let go of my hand, causing my heart to race. "Dinner Saturday night, then?"

"I'm looking forward to it already."

***

I smoothed down my dress, a simple black sheath, for the hundredth time as I paced back and forth in front of the door. I'd realized this was my first romantic date since moving to this town, and my nerves jittered in anticipation. It had been so long since I'd stepped out of the role of an assistant prosecutor, a professional career woman. Tonight, Alex would see me as a person outside of my position.

The buzzer sounded and I pushed the button. A minute later, he knocked at the door. I tugged at the hem of the dress one final time and reached for the handle.

Alex beamed at me from the other side of the threshold. "Wow," he said. "You look...wow."

"Likewise," I said, taking in his crisp button-down shirt and slim-fitting slacks. I grabbed my purse from the table and shut the door behind me. "Did you have any problems finding my building?"

"I've encountered far more challenging investigations." He offered me his arm, and I looped my hand through his elbow. "Come on. I'm parked right outside."

I let him escort me to the elevator, where we waited for it to arrive on my floor. "I turned that file you gave me over to Hayes, the phone records and everything," I said. "On Monday, he's going to—"

"Shh." Alex put a finger to his lips. "I meant it when I said no work-related conversation tonight. No crimes, no trials, none of the darker side of society...I just want to spend a pleasant evening with a beautiful woman and not have to worry about any of that."

I blushed and offered him a sheepish grin. "Sorry."

"It's okay. I've fallen into that trap more times than I can count."

We descended into the lobby and exited the building. He opened the passenger side door for me and I slid inside his car. Once we were on our way, I felt the stresses of the prior weeks easing out of my neck and shoulders. Even if nothing came of this date, I was glad for the temporary distraction.

"Have you been to this place before?" Alex asked as we approached the restaurant.

"Nope. Just driven past it a few times."

He put the car in park and walked around to open the door for me again. I appreciated the chivalrous gesture. "Everything I've ever had here is pretty good," he continued. "Some people claim you can't get great food outside of the city, but I have no complaints."

"I trust your judgment." I patted his arm to reassure him and was rewarded by the feel of a firm, sculpted bicep beneath my hand. Nice. "Do you get down there very often?"

"When I can. My mom and some of my brothers and sisters still live in the Bronx, but as you and I have already established, sometimes work gets in the way of everything else."

The hostess showed us to a cozy table in the back corner of the room. After pulling my chair out, Alex sat adjacent to me rather than on the opposite side. "I didn't know you weren't originally from around here," I said, letting a coy smile twist up one side of my mouth. "Now I'm worried I won't seem interesting enough to someone who's spent so much time in such an exciting place."

He laughed. "Don't be ridiculous. I can't think of a single woman I've met anywhere else that I'd rather be here with tonight." Leaning toward me, his leg brushed against mine. "What about you? Where did you spend your days before gracing this small town with your captivating presence?"

"Upstate. Very upstate. Like, Canada was at the end of the street upstate."

The conversation flowed freely, to the point where we ignored our menus until the waiter suggested we place an order. I'd been eating, sleeping, and breathing the Lattimer case for so long, I couldn't remember the last time I relaxed and thought about anything else. The company of such a handsome, charming man didn't hurt, either.

"I can't believe the time," Alex said when the waiter nudged the bill in his direction. "I didn't mean to keep you out so late."

"I don't mind at all. I don't have to work

tomorrow."

"Good. But still, I should be getting you home." He took his wallet out of his pocket and flagged down our server.

The ride back to my apartment seemed to fly by. I didn't want the evening to end, and anticipation twisted in my stomach as I thought about all the possibilities that awaited us. As expected, my date walked me all the way to my doorstep. "I'm so glad we had this opportunity to get to know each other," he said. "Ever since the first case we worked together, I wanted to learn more about you."

I stood facing him and gazed up into his eyes. His muscular frame towered over me, and I was very aware of the close proximity of my body to his. "I always did enjoy whenever we'd run into each other. I don't know why we didn't do this sooner."

"Me too." He tucked a lock of hair back behind my ear, and his thumb grazed my cheek, making my nerves tingle with excitement. "But let's not worry about that. I just want to think about moving forward from here."

Tilting my face upward, I welcomed the incoming kiss. Alex's lips pressed against mine, soft, warm, and inviting. My breath hitched in my throat as he wove his fingers through my hair, holding me in place. I parted my mouth to let our tongues mingle, and the taste of him left me weak in the knees.

Like the rest of the evening, the kiss was over far too soon. The words tumbled out of me before I could stop them. "Would you like to come inside?" I whispered, feeling the heat rise to my face.

A faint groan rumbled from his chest. "More than anything." He leaned his head against the door frame and sighed. "But not tonight."

My brow furrowed, but he continued before I said anything further. "I don't want to rush things with you, Celeste." He took my hand in his and squeezed. "You're a special woman and I want to do this right." The dazzling grin that had won over my heart reappeared. "Besides, my mother always told me to be a gentleman."

I giggled and straightened the collar of his shirt. "Your mother would be proud."

Alex raised our intertwined fingers to his mouth and kissed them. "We'll do this again real soon. I promise."

Standing on my toes, I swiped my lips across his cheek before opening my door. "Good night."

Weeks passed as the DA's office moved forward with preparing for the trial. Although I dutifully did what was asked of me, the question of Nick Lattimer's guilt plagued me. Outside of work, I had a series of similar dates with the delectable Alex Delgado, but time spent with him did little to calm me down. His casual touches and lingering looks drove me wild, yet we'd done nothing beyond those deep, fervent kisses that left me wanting more.

I didn't know whether he was intentionally trying to tease me, to cultivate a borderline obsession with him. Whatever his plans were, they were working. Thoughts of him consumed all my free moments. I dreamed of his body pressed against mine, his hands and mouth exploring every inch of my skin. Between prepping for the trial, despite my misgivings, and picturing the detective in all sorts of compromising positions, I spent many sleepless nights wide awake in my bed. Something had to give.

Just when I thought I was going to snap like an overly-stretched rubber band, Colin summoned me to his office. He still held his phone to his ear when I arrived at his door, but he beckoned me inside with his other hand. "Thanks for letting us know," he said into the receiver. "Send over a copy of the paperwork whenever you're done tying up all your loose ends." Though his voice was cordial, a strange look darkened his face as he hung up the phone, one I couldn't quite read.

"What's going on?" I asked, taking a seat in an empty chair.

"That was the Manhattan DA's office. They're finally breaking up this drug ring they've been after for years, having turned some of its members." He rubbed his temples with his thumb and forefinger. "In exchange for a better deal and sentences served concurrently rather than consecutively, it seems one of the crimes that has been confessed to is the murder of one Miss Sherri Strahan."

I let out a long breath. "Let me guess. The confessor is someone other than Nick Lattimer."

"You are correct."

An uncomfortable silence hung in the room as I mulled over this new information. "Did this other person really do it?"

"He knew details we withheld from the press, so if he didn't, he at least knows who did." Colin ran his hand through his hair and paced back and forth in front of his desk. "You know, I thought Lattimer was guilty as hell and we were going to get a conviction. That I was so off base is...unsettling."

"We did the best we could based on the evidence we had. Isn't that what you told me?"

"Yes, but I don't like being reminded of how our system has its flaws." He leaned back against the desk, shoulders slumped, and looked over at me. "Thank you, Celeste. Were it not for your careful work, this office could have imprisoned an innocent man."

"I'm glad it didn't come to that." I stood and took a step closer to him. "Are you all right?"

Colin offered me a tired smile, his eyes crinkling at the corners. "I'll be fine. The system did work, after all." He gestured toward the door. "It's already late in the afternoon and I'm sure the judges are gone for the day. Let's leave this mess for tomorrow and we'll work on our motions as soon as we get what we need from Manhattan."

I left the room feeling as if a giant weight had been lifted from my shoulders. This job rarely had its slow moments, but at least I could complete my remaining work with a clear conscience. When I returned to my office, I grabbed my cell phone out of my pocketbook and ducked into the break room. Might as well see if I could take advantage of my good fortune, I thought.

"Hey there," Alex said when he answered my call.

"Hey yourself. You'll never guess what just happened." I quickly filled him in on the details.

He whistled. "So, you were right after all."

"*We* were right. I wouldn't have been able to do anything without your help." I grinned, even though I knew he couldn't see me. "Let's celebrate tonight."

"What did you have in mind?"

Oh, if you only knew. "Why don't you come over to my place around seven?" I suggested. "I'll make my famous linguine with clam sauce."

Alex laughed, a deep, throaty sound that made my heart skip a beat. "I'd be an idiot to turn down that offer."

"I'll see you later, then."

I stopped at the grocery store on the way home to gather the necessary supplies. Once I had the sauce simmering on the stove, I went down the checklist to get myself ready. I shaved my legs, ran a brush through my hair, and stood in front of the dresser, faced with the contents of my underwear drawer. Tucked in the back recesses lay a bright red satin bra with a matching thong that revealed more than it covered. Neither had seen the light of day for longer than I cared to admit, but as I held them up in front of me, the choice was clear.

With my breasts pushed up practically to my chin, I pulled a pair of jeans and a gauzy sweater out of the closet. I didn't have long to adjust the deep V neckline before the buzzer rang. Fluffing out my hair as I hurried toward the door, I slammed the button with more force than expected. *Calm down,* I told myself. *Let's not appear too...eager.*

Alex soon appeared, holding a bouquet of wildflowers in one hand and a bottle of white wine in the other. "It smells amazing in here," he said, forgoing any polite greeting.

"Thanks." I led him into the kitchen and handed him a corkscrew and two glasses before digging around in a cabinet for a vase. "It's been a while since I've cooked like this, but I figured tonight was as good of an occasion as any."

"I won't argue!" He opened the bottle with a loud pop. "Can I help you with anything?"

"Absolutely not. Just sit there and drink your wine, and I'll finish up the pasta."

Smirking, he gave me a mock salute before sliding into a chair. "Yes, ma'am."

I worked my way around the kitchen, wondering if I was imagining his eyes tracking my every move. Dinner was ready at the scheduled time, but I was too anxious to eat more than a few bites. I pushed the food around the plate and hoped our conversation was enough to prevent him from noticing my lack of appetite.

"I'll take care of the dishes later," I said when he'd finished. Picking up my glass of wine, I headed for the sofa. "Now that you're fed, it's time to finally unwind."

"You deserve it." Alex took a seat next to me. We set our glasses on the coffee table, and then I curled up against his side when he leaned back. "Crazy how that case worked out after all, huh?"

Resting my head on his shoulder, I nestled into the space beneath his arm. "I thought we weren't supposed to talk about work at times like this," I teased.

He chuckled. "Our jobs are part of who we are. Sometimes there's no fighting it." His grip on me tightened as he gave me a playful squeeze. "Besides, justice was served. It's always nice when the good guys win for a change."

The warmth of his skin and the effects of the wine lulled me into a state of pleasant serenity. "We do make a pretty good team, don't we?"

"The best crime-fighting duo this side of the Hudson, as far as I'm concerned."

"Just think of all we could do together." I shifted so I could gaze up at him. Mere inches separated his face from mine. "The possibilities are endless."

Cupping my cheek, Alex kissed me, long and slow. I lazily swirled my tongue around his, savoring the taste of him. It should have been the perfect end to a pretty good day, yet

I wasn't satisfied. I needed more.

"Stay with me tonight," I murmured against his lips. "I can't stand one more night without you."

He drew back to look at me with half-lidded eyes. "Are you sure? I don't want you to think I'm only after one thing here."

"You've already won me over with your sweet gestures and good intentions. Long ago, in fact." Emboldened by the day's successes and a couple of glasses of pinot grigio, I slid one leg over his lap, straddling him. "Make me yours."

Our decadent, luxurious kisses bloomed into something more fervent. Alex's hands slipped inside my sweater and skimmed my bare back. I arched and ground against him, feeling his erection expanding beneath me. A faint moan reverberated through my lips.

His palms roamed across my skin, leaving fiery trails in their wake. When he reached my satin-encased breasts, I gasped. He brushed his thumbs over my nipples, and I writhed in his lap. Every time I moved, his thick cock rubbed against me through our clothing.

I finally broke the kiss to raise my arms over my head. He pulled my sweater up and off, leaving my cleavage exposed to him at eye-level. He smiled and let out that deep laugh that always made my insides melt. "I should have known you were hiding something beneath all those prim and proper suits," he said, running his finger along the edge of the scarlet fabric. "Scandalous. I love it."

I blushed brighter than the color of the satin and made a mental note to consider similar purchases in the future. "And what about you?" My fingertips danced up the front of his shirt until I tugged at his collar. "When does my imagination get satisfied?"

"Not here." He let go of my bra and grinned up at me. "Because if we're not careful, we'll wind up spending the night out here on the couch, and I think we can do better."

I laughed and slid off his legs. "The bedroom's that way," I said, pointing.

"Excellent."

Alex stood up. In one swift motion, he scooped me into his strong arms and carried me in the direction I'd indicated. Giggling, I clung to his broad shoulders as we entered my room. He set me down on the bed, flung back the covers, and then attacked my mouth for another heated kiss.

I leaned back against the pillows and pulled him down on top of me. The weight of him pressing me into the mattress felt divine. His lips traveled to the side of my neck, where he licked and nibbled a path over the delicate skin. I struggled to breathe evenly, losing myself in the feathery sensations.

When he pushed one bra strap off my shoulder, I stopped him. "Come on, Detective, this isn't fair." I yanked at his shirt again, freeing the hem from the top of his pants. "Let me see the results of all that fitness training they make you do."

Flashing that devilish smile once more, he indulged my desire. He sat up and whipped off the shirt, flinging it to the floor. Enough moonlight streamed in through the shades to illuminate the chiseled muscles of his chest and arms. Unable to resist, I reached out and traced a line around one well-defined pec. The sight before me was better than I ever could have imagined.

Skin met skin as he returned to my side. Warmth spread throughout my core when we made contact, and he turned his focus back to my heaving breasts. I squirmed beneath him as he peppered my chest with fluttery kisses, but he held me in place. Reaching behind me, he unclasped the bra, finally freeing me.

Sparks shot through me when his mouth closed over one hardened nipple. A whimper left my lips. His teeth grazed over the erect bud and another rush of arousal flooded my body. I was torn between wanting to savor his deliberate teasing and soothing the ache building between my legs.

Alex let my breast fall from his mouth to attend to its mate. I ran my fingers through his hair, my body rising to meet his. He folded his arms around my waist and continued to lave attention upon my chest.

Just when I thought I couldn't take anymore, he loosened his hold on me. Relief was short-lived, as he kissed a path over my stomach, taking his time proceeding lower and lower. Nimble fingers unfastened my jeans, and he jerked them off over my hips.

"A matching set," he said, skimming his finger over the damp triangle of fabric. His breath danced across my cleft and I thought I might explode right then. "I shouldn't have expected anything less with your attention to detail."

My legs trembled around him. Enough was enough. "You're going to make me beg, aren't you?"

He kissed my inner thigh. "Don't worry, Celeste." Little by little he pulled the thong down and off. "I'll take care of you. I promise."

At long last, he lapped at the entrance of my pussy. I moaned and my hips jerked toward him of their own volition. He painted wide strokes with his tongue, probing inside me. My fists knotted in the sheets and my head rolled from side to side, but there was no escape from his expert manipulations. His palms cupped my ass, holding me in position as his mouth worked me into a state of frenzy.

Pleasure coiled in my muscles, making my breaths come in short pants. Eyes closed, I murmured his name, pleading with him to rid my body of all the stress and anxiety that had plagued me for weeks. Acquiescing to my demands once more, he sucked down hard on my clit. The tip of his tongue circled around the sensitive nub with skilled precision, sending me spiraling into an amazing climax.

I thrashed on the bed, letting the power of the orgasm consume me. Tension flowed out of me as if someone had pulled the plug on a drain, and I felt light and free. When I could control my movements again, I reached down to stroke the side of Alex's face. He shifted until he was next to me, propped up on one elbow. The way he beamed at me sent a fresh wave of bliss coursing through my soul.

"I hope that was worth the wait," he said, twirling a lock of my hair in his fingers.

"It was." Now that I was no longer gasping

for air, I could concentrate more on him. I let my hand drop until it rested on the solid bulge beneath his zipper. "But we're not done yet."

"Not at all."

Alex stood beside the bed, his body framed by the moonlit window. I curled up on my side to watch him remove his pants, exposing more lean muscles and creamy brown skin. His boxer shorts followed and I got my first glimpse of his engorged cock. That longing ache in my pussy stirred again.

He draped his pants over the chair in the corner. Before he returned to me, he retrieved his wallet from the pocket and pulled something out. I rolled back and laughed when I saw the wrapped condom in his hands. "So much for your noble intentions!"

He shrugged, though the mischievous glint was ever present in his eyes. "What can I say? It's always good to be prepared for anything."

"Such a Boy Scout."

Lying down next to me, he brushed a few sweaty strands of hair away from my face. I could smell my own arousal on his lips, and it only further incited my lust. Hunger wracked my mind and body. I had to have him.

I turned toward him and reached between us. His cock felt heavy and swollen in my hand, and I ran my fingers up and down its length. He was more than ready for me, but I couldn't help giving him a few light pumps.

His dick throbbed, and he groaned. "I know I said I didn't want to rush, but—"

"Then what are you waiting for?" I kissed him, tasting the tangy juices. On his tongue, they were intoxicating. "I need you inside me."

Alex opened the condom and pressed it into my palm. I rolled it down his thick shaft, cupping his balls when I got to the bottom. He bit back another groan as he positioned himself between my knees.

I inhaled sharply when his tip penetrated me. He advanced at an agonizing pace, taking his time embedding his cock to the hilt. Inch by magnificent inch, I took him in, my pussy enveloping him as if we were made for each other. Sighing, I closed my eyes to better memorize the perfect moment.

His mouth swept across mine in a faint kiss. "Let me watch you," he whispered, caressing my cheek.

I opened my eyes to meet his dreamy stare, and he pushed forward. With long, slow thrusts, he filled me, plunging deep inside. I matched his movements, bucking up to meet him. My legs curled around his waist to draw him farther in. Our gazes locked together, we settled into a steady rhythm.

Each time our bodies collided, another wild thrill pulsed in my veins. I gripped his arms to brace myself, but I was on the brink of losing control yet again. His cock drove into me with increasing force. I dug my fingertips into his rigid muscles and let him take command.

Beads of sweat dotted his brow. He was getting close. My thighs tightened around him and I pulled his head down close to mine. "Come for me," I demanded, nipping at his lower lip.

Alex slammed into my cunt so hard, I thought the bed would collapse beneath us. I wouldn't have cared, though, as the onslaught shoved me into a second orgasm. My face buried in his shoulder, I clung to him, letting our shared ecstasy course through my bloodstream and sing in my heart.

His head landed on the pillow beside mine. Once he disposed of the condom, he wrapped his arms around me. I reached for the covers to tug them over our entwined bodies. Nestled against him, I felt warm and safe and free of all worries. Everything felt *right*.

"That was incredible," he said, kissing my temple.

"Definitely." My eyelids drooped and I leaned my head on his chest. "We do make a pretty good team."

"The best." His pulse thumped in my ear in a reassuring rhythm. As I drifted off to sleep, I heard his last murmured words. "And I can't wait to fall further in love with you."

***

After what seemed like an interminably long winter, spring rolled around. I couldn't say I minded the cozy nights spent cuddling next to Alex, but I was glad for the return of warmer weather. With the golden sunshine and budding flowers came some more significant, personal changes.

The DA's office dismissed all charges against Nick Lattimer. Whether or not he was actually guilty of murder, none of us could ever be one hundred percent sure. Regardless, I still felt relief that we hadn't risked convicting an innocent man. In my heart, I didn't believe he had killed Sherri Strahan. I trusted my instincts and felt satisfied with the results.

My contributions to the case didn't go unnoticed by the higher-ups at work. Due to my attention to detail and growing confidence, I received a promotion. The hours were long and my caseload still never-ending, but it was work I enjoyed. Even though the system wasn't completely failsafe, I loved being a prosecutor. As time passed, my responsibilities kept increasing. Before long, I took the lead on some trials and worked to build my success rate.

Lastly, my relationship with Alex deepened and flourished. Every experience with him felt new and exciting, yet in some ways, it felt like we'd been together for years. He fit into my life so comfortably, I couldn't imagine ever being without him. Our first wonderful night together led to many more until barely a morning went by when we didn't wake up in each other's arms. I was the first to suggest sharing a living space, but he insisted such an arrangement needed to come with at least an engagement ring. Luckily, I agreed autumn in upstate New York would provide the perfect backdrop to a small, intimate wedding.

Although we tried to distinguish our professional selves from our lives at home, he'd been right when he'd said they couldn't truly be separated. The pursuit of justice was an integral part of who we were, and it was one of the many, many things I loved about him. Our jobs were different, but we were on the same side, striving to achieve the same goals. As we planned our future together, I had faith in our shared power to shape our world for the better. What more could I ask for?

A SECRET SONG

I had already given up hope of ever returning to my nice, cozy apartment that night. "I'll meet you there," I said to Delgado. "I might as well hear what this guy has to say firsthand."

It was a short drive over to the stationhouse, barely enough to let the car's heat warm my hands. The detectives had arrived before me and escorted Nick Lattimer inside while I braced myself for the next shock of cold air and tried not to fantasize about a fancy cappuccino. I hurried to the door, where I met Captain Redding, an older woman who I'd always gotten along with in our brief encounters. She appeared just as displeased at being dragged out of bed in the middle of the night as I'm sure I did, but she offered me a tired smile. "At least it's not snowing," she said as she walked with me toward one of the interrogation rooms.

"True. But then there might have been footprints leading us directly to the killer."

She laughed. "You haven't been around here long enough to be this jaded."

"I'm sure I'll be more cheery tomorrow." I wrinkled my nose. "Or in a few days, rather, considering it's tomorrow already."

We stood at the two-way mirror to observe the detectives question Mr. Lattimer. I prepared to jump in and stop the interrogation at the first mention of invoking his right to counsel, but he was adamant he didn't need to consult an attorney. "I didn't do it," he said. "I didn't kill Sherri."

"They all sing the same old song," Captain Redding said, shaking her head.

I stared through the glass. "What do you think so far?"

"I don't know." She shrugged her shoulders. "Not all the evidence is in yet, and it's too soon to get a good read off him either way."

We listened to Lattimer answer the detectives' questions, and I tried to get a clearer picture of his character and note any inconsistencies. Yes, he'd known Sherri Strahan. No, he wasn't aware they lived in the same apartment complex. Yes, she'd testified against his brother. No, he hadn't seen her that night. Back and forth they went, and he told the same story without any variations.

I stifled a yawn and resisted the urge to check the time on my phone. "Mind if I step out for a couple minutes and steal a cup of coffee?"

"Not at all. I'll be here." The captain waved me off. "I apologize in advance for the quality of that sludge."

I wandered down the hallway to the break room, where a half-full pot of coffee sat on its warmer. Two packets of sugar made it taste more palatable and I gulped it down. The chances of returning home before reporting to the office seemed slim, so I poured myself a second cup to take with me.

The fluorescent lights glared overhead in the narrow corridor, and I rubbed my eyes with my free hand as I headed back to the interrogation room. When I opened my eyes again, I found myself about to walk straight into Nick Lattimer. "Excuse me," I mumbled.

He didn't let me pass. "You were there, at my apartment," he said, taking a step closer. "You're not a cop, though."

I glanced past him and saw the detectives at the other end of the hallway watching us. "No, I'm not. I'm with the DA's office."

"Ah. A lawyer." His hazel eyes looked me up and down. "Nice."

I tried not to squirm beneath his intense gaze. "Mr. Lattimer, I'm not sure we should be speaking with each other like this."

"Why? I have nothing to hide." His brow furrowed.

"Given the circumstances, I don't think it's...appropriate."

Full lips curled into a smirk. "Well, I'd hate for you to engage in *inappropriate* behavior on my behalf."

Flustered, I tried to come up with a suitable response and failed. Before I could say anything, Detective Delgado strode down the hallway and positioned himself between us. "Sorry, I should have been more specific in my directions to the men's room," he said cheerfully. "Let me show you the way."

I made my escape as they proceeded in the opposite direction and returned to Captain Redding. "Guess we all needed a break," I said.

"He hasn't given us anything useful yet." She drummed her fingers against the edge of the mirror. "We might be here for a while."

The men came back and the questioning resumed. Lattimer's jaw tightened when the topic turned to his brother, yet he kept his answers straightforward and polite. Similarly, the detectives showed no signs of letting up in their interrogation. Someone had to crack eventually, and I wasn't sure which side it would be.

Chaos erupted at six o'clock on the dot, when several things happened all at once. "This is getting ridiculous," Lattimer said. The force with which he stood up sent his chair skidding backward into the wall. "I don't know what else I can tell you, and I'd really like to go home now."

My cell phone rang again. "Celeste? What is going on over there?" Hints of annoyance tempered Colin's voice. "I expected to hear from you by now."

As I filled him in on what had happened since arriving at the police station, two more officers entered the room. They spoke with Captain Redding, whose eyebrow shot up at whatever they told her, and she looked over at me. "Hold on one second," I said into the phone.

"They came from the crime scene," the

captain told me. "And they found a bloody knife in a garbage can behind Nick Lattimer's unit. We won't know if it's Sherri Strahan's blood until the tests come back, but...."

"Right." I turned my attention back to the phone. "I don't know if you heard any of that, but what could possibly be the murder weapon just turned up near Lattimer's apartment."

"Hmm." Colin sighed. "Between this discovery and the thing with his brother, it's enough. I don't want this guy disappearing on us."

"Got it. I'll see you in a couple hours."

Lattimer paced back and forth behind the table. "You can't just keep me here like this," he said, moving toward the door. "I'm leaving."

That was my cue. I entered the room; now it was my turn to block his path. For a fleeting moment, our gazes locked together. His gold-flecked eyes burned into me and my breath caught in my throat.

"Miss McConnell?" Delgado said, shattering the growing tension.

I looked away and swallowed. "Arrest him."

***

The sun had already dipped below the horizon when I left the office after five o'clock. Dingy clouds muddled the sky, coloring everything below an unpleasant shade of gray. "I hate winter," I mumbled, tugging on the front of my coat as I exited the building.

My car sat at the far end of the parking lot. As I rifled through my bag for my keys, I noticed someone leaning against the front. I squinted into the distance, and a chill rolled down my spine when I recognized who was waiting for me.

Nick Lattimer.

I froze, my eyes darting around to see if anyone else was nearby. We were the only two people in the lot. I tried to surreptitiously retrieve my cell phone in case I needed to summon help, though I wasn't sure exactly what I was afraid of.

He noticed my movements and put his hands up in the universal non-threatening gesture. "I'm not going to hurt you," he said. "I just wanted to talk."

In the back of my mind, I remembered Colin being in a bad mood when he'd learned the judge had granted Lattimer bail. I hadn't given much thought about whether or not he should be released until now. "I can't see what we could possibly have to talk about," I said, standing in place. "And how did you know which car was mine?"

"From the night that...well, you know."

I crossed my arms over my chest. "It still doesn't answer the question of why you want to talk to *me* of all people."

He ran his hand through his dark blond hair and sighed. "Because I didn't kill Sherri and I need to find a way to prove it."

"Mr. Lattimer, I—"

"Nick." He looked at me through the strands of hair that had fallen back over his brow. "Call me Nick."

I sighed. "Nick, I don't know what you expect me to do. This is a conversation you should be having with your own attorney."

"Yeah, okay." He snorted and rolled his eyes. "That idiot from Legal Aid is worth exactly what I'm paying him. All he does is try to convince me to take a plea bargain so he can move on to his next case as soon as possible."

Recalling the lawyer that had been assigned to him, I couldn't disagree with his assessment. However, part of me knew this conversation wasn't appropriate for someone in my position. We stood and stared at each other in the secluded parking lot, locked in a stalemate.

I broke the silence first. "What do you want from me?" I asked quietly.

Nick's expression softened. "Just listen to what I have to say. No one, not even my useless lawyer, has heard my side of the story yet."

"Fine." A cold wind whipped through my hair and I yanked at my coat again. "But not here. And not anywhere too...private."

He nodded. "Fair enough. How about the diner over on Washington? I could go for something to eat, anyway."

I pulled my keys out of my bag. "I'll meet you over there."

During the drive to the small restaurant at

the outskirts of town, I continued to question my decision. Discussing Nick's case in a public place removed much of the potential for danger, yet I had other concerns. What if this was all a ploy, a manipulation tactic to bolster his defense by claiming impropriety from the prosecution? Was I risking my job by meeting with him? But on the other hand, what if he really was innocent of this gruesome crime? Could I help send him to prison without knowing for sure?

I sat at a booth inside the diner and shrugged off my coat. Nick arrived moments later and slid in across from me. "Start talking," I said. "And this had better be good."

"Look, I know all the evidence you have against me, and how your office is going to spin it to a jury. Hell, I'd probably believe it if I were one of them." He folded his hands in front of him. "But here's the thing. I had no reason to want Sherri dead, no motive to kill her."

I raised an eyebrow. "Her testimony helped convict your brother on all sorts of drug charges, and you're telling me you have zero problem with that?"

"Pretty much." His full lips curved downward and darkness clouded his eyes. "I love my brother and I miss seeing him all the time, but when he went to jail, it was a wake-up call for me. I realized I was headed down the same path, and it's not what I wanted my life to be."

A waitress came by to fill our coffee cups and I took a long sip. "That's a nice story. I hope your lawyer tells it as convincingly at trial."

"I'm serious. Why do you think I moved up here?" He brushed his hair to the side again and leaned forward. "I did some things I'm not proud of, okay? I wanted to get away from all the people who would drag me back into those messes. I wanted a fresh start."

"And you just so happened to wind up in the same apartment complex as the victim?"

"I know you probably won't believe this...." Nick shrugged, but maintained eye contact. "I didn't even know Sherri lived there until that night. It's a big place and I'd never seen her."

I stirred a little more creamer into my mug and tried to sound indifferent. "That is a pretty big stretch. What about the knife the police found in your garbage can, the one covered in the victim's blood?"

He didn't flinch. "Did they find my fingerprints on it?"

"...No."

"And do you really think I'm *that* stupid?" He flashed me that coy half-smile. "If I were to kill anyone, I mean."

He did make some valid points, I admitted to myself. Possibly even enough to create reasonable doubt in the minds of the jury. I lifted the cup to take another sip. "If not you, then who?"

For the first time since we'd sat down, he glanced away from me. "I have some ideas, but I don't want to say too much yet."

I let out an exasperated sigh and set the coffee cup down on the saucer with a loud clank. "So, why me? Why don't you go to the police?"

Nick shook his head. "The cops don't care. They think their job is complete and turned it over to you guys. They're done." His chin jutted out. "One way or another, I'm going to find a way to prove I'm innocent. And I could use all the help I can get."

I said nothing.

"Just consider it, okay?" He reached over the table and let his fingers rest on my wrist. My breath caught in my throat, but I didn't pull away. "I know you work for the DA's office," he said, "but don't you want to find the truth? Isn't that the best way to get justice for Sherri?"

"Maybe." I bit my lower lip and tried not to think too much about how his hand felt on mine. "Give me a day or two to think about everything you've told me."

"Of course." He shifted to one side to take something out of his pocket. Producing a pen, he took a clean napkin from the stack on the table and scribbled something on it. "Here's my cell phone number. Call me any time."

I tucked the napkin inside my bag and slid my cup and saucer toward the center of the table. The inexplicable flutters in my stomach erased any appetite I'd had, and I needed time to myself to sort through all that had transpired. "I should go," I said, picking up my purse and coat.

Nick watched me stand. "I'm going to get something to eat here. I promise I'm not going to follow you home or anything."

My eyes widened.

"Sorry." He offered me a sheepish grin. "I guess I need to work on my efforts to convince you I'm not the dangerous criminal a lot of people think I am."

"Yeah, well...."

I was almost past his side of the booth when he reached out and grabbed my arm. "Thank you for agreeing to come here." Glimmering hazel eyes gazed up at me as heat spread over my skin. "I didn't know where else to turn, and I thought you might...." His hand dropped and he turned his attention to the menu in front of him. "Never mind. I'll let you leave."

I hurried out of the diner, my heart racing.

For the rest of the night, I replayed the conversations with Nick in my head, as well as the facts of the case. The questions I'd asked myself on the way to our meeting resurfaced, and I still didn't have any good answers. Had he lulled Sherri into a false sense of security with his charisma and sympathetic words before murdering her? Or was he being framed for this brutal crime? As I tossed and turned in bed, I waited for a solution to this dilemma to flash through my mind, but none came.

To agree to help Nick find the evidence he needs, turn to Page 103.

OR

To share concerns and doubts with Detective Delgado, turn to Page 51.

BAD GIRL

Dragging myself into work the following morning was difficult, and not just because of the lack of sleep. I may have been employed by the DA's office, the entity responsible for prosecuting Nick Lattimer, but I felt a sense of duty to a higher power. In addition to the desire for justice, I admittedly felt a little thrill when I thought about any covert activities I'd be participating in. All my life I'd played by the rules, been the stereotypical "good girl" who always did what was expected of her. Now I'd be consorting with an accused murderer with a checkered past. An *attractive* accused murderer with a checkered past.

I waited until I was out of the office to call the number on the napkin from the diner. "Nick?" I asked when someone picked up the phone.

"Yeah?"

"It's Celeste McConnell. From the DA's office."

"Oh." He paused. "I didn't think you were actually going to call me."

"I've been thinking a lot about the case." I took a deep breath. "I want to help you."

"Wow. I mean, uh, that's great. Really." He sounded genuinely surprised. "Do you want to meet up sometime to talk about our next steps?"

My hand holding the phone grew clammy. "Yes, but we have to be careful. No one knows I'm doing this, and it probably wouldn't look good if anyone from work saw me with you."

If Nick was offended by my concerns, he didn't say anything about it. "Well, you already know where I live...."

Heat flooded my cheeks and I couldn't believe the words about to come out of my mouth. "I'll be over in an hour."

At the designated time, I knocked on Nick's door with a trembling hand. He opened it and moved to the side. "Come on in."

I entered, unsure if I was stepping into a dangerous situation. He closed the door behind me, and I noted he didn't lock it. When he plopped onto the sofa, I gingerly sat on an armchair opposite him, keeping a safe distance.

He looked me over from head to toe across the scuffed coffee table. "I didn't lure you here to hurt you or anything," he said. "You can relax."

I remained sitting with my back straight and my purse on my lap. "There's nothing wrong with being cautious."

"Mm-hmm." His eyes narrowed. "Part of

you still thinks there's a chance I might have killed Sherri."

He wasn't wrong, but I'd come here for a reason. "Maybe." I leaned back against the cushions and crossed my legs. "So, convince me otherwise. What didn't you tell me at the diner?"

Nick matched my reclined position and propped one foot up on the opposite knee. "Sherri testified against my brother when she was caught selling drugs. She was smart enough to take a deal, where my brother wasn't." Sighing, he shook his head. "Though in retrospect, maybe it wasn't the best move, considering she was killed on the outside."

I leaned against the side of the chair and rested my chin in my hand. "What sort of deal did your brother turn down?"

"Jeremy provided some people—yes, myself included—with some stuff to sell. But he had to get it from somewhere, right?" He drummed his fingers on the edge of his sneaker. "It's this whole huge organization in the city, and it's run by this guy named

Frankie. I only met him a couple times, but I could tell he's very smart. He has to be, if he's been doing this for so long without having any charges against him stick."

"And your brother refused to name him?"

"Yup. So, he's sitting in jail." His lips twisted into a wry smile. "I guess he thought better alive in there than dead out here. Can't really argue with that logic."

I frowned. "And I suppose I can't talk you into telling the police all of this?"

Nick's brow furrowed. "Tell them what? I don't have any evidence or proof of anything Frankie's done, and they already think I'm a murderer."

Seeing the criminal justice system from a different perspective was a little unnerving. I tried to change the subject. "But you think this Frankie is the one who killed Sherri?"

"More like instructed someone to do it."

"I don't understand." I shifted to the other side of the armchair. "Why would he kill her? Furthermore, why would he kill her and not you?"

"Hell if I know. It would look awfully suspicious if we both turned up dead." He rubbed his eyes with the heels of his hands. "Sherri testified against one of his associates and needed to be punished. I tried to get away from all of this, but he's teaching me there's no escape. Framing me for murder is one way to tie up some loose ends."

Nick's theories made sense, but he was right. There was no proof. "Let's say I believe you," I said. "What's your plan? What do you want *me* to do?"

"I was going to do some digging, go down to the city and talk to a few friends to start with." He leaned forward, his elbows on his knees. "And I was thinking you could come with me. Be another set of ears, as well as offering some legal advice if necessary."

Every cell in my brain screamed this was a bad idea, but I'd already made a decision. And even if I hadn't, the way Nick looked at me with his smoldering gaze, plus the pleas that came from those full lips would have made it difficult for me to resist. "Okay," I said.

"Excellent." He grinned. "We'll take a little trip down to a club in Manhattan next Saturday night. I'll drive."

"I suppose that'll be the ultimate test as to whether I still think you're going to drag me off and kill me."

Nick laughed, the first genuine laugh I'd heard since we'd met. It was a pleasant sound. "I guess so. Oh, and one other thing."

"What?"

He looked me over again, slowly this time, letting his gaze linger on my body. I swallowed hard, anticipating what he would say. "If we're going to a nightclub, you might want to wear something other than a sweater and baggy jeans. You know, you don't want to stand out for the wrong reasons."

A flush of warmth rose to my cheeks. "I'll see what I can find in my closet. It's been a while since I went out anywhere like that." I glanced away. "A long while."

He chuckled. "I guess you didn't take a lot of study breaks in law school."

"No, not really."

"It seems to have worked out well for you." Behind the sandy strands of his hair, a devilish glint lit up his eyes. "But everyone needs to let loose every now and then. I think Saturday will be good for both of us."

***

It was already dark by the time I arrived at Nick's apartment for our drive to the city. "Nice makeup," he said, shutting the door behind him. "Let's go."

We got into his car and pulled out of the parking lot. The drive to Manhattan took just over an hour, and we spent much of the time discussing me, for a change. I talked about my decision to pursue a career in law, answering any questions he asked. Gradually, the topics of conversation became more personal, and we spoke of our lives before each of us moved to our quiet little town. As we shared stories and laughed together, it was easy to forget the circumstances that had introduced us, or what we were about to attempt.

Nick parked in a garage and we stepped out into the illuminated street. Though the city was usually warmer than the suburbs, the cold air still pierced through my coat, and I shivered as we hurried along the sidewalk. "How many blocks away is this place?" I asked through chattering teeth.

He untied his scarf and handed it to me. "Only two more."

When we arrived at our destination, there was a line to get into the club. "Fantastic," I mumbled as I prepared for my nose to freeze off.

Taking my arm to guide me, Nick strode past the crowd to the bouncer by the door. "Nick! Long time, no see!" the man greeted him, grinning.

"Haven't been in the city much lately." Nick matched his cheery expression. "But I couldn't come here without saying hello to all my friends."

"It's good to see you. Try not to get into too much trouble." The bouncer winked as he opened the door and let us pass.

We entered the building. "I didn't know you were so well-connected," I said.

"I admit I used to do a lot of business here." He laughed. "And I always tipped well, which might account for how I stayed under the police's radar for so long."

"I'll pretend I'm not hearing any of this."

Nick walked up to the coat check and handed his jacket to the woman behind the counter. I shrugged out of my coat and did the same. "Well, well, well," he said, chuckling. His eyes traveled up and down my body, glittering in the wan lighting. "I guess all my concerns about blending in were for nothing."

"Oh, stop." Heat spread over my face, down my neck and across my chest. I'd stood in front of my closet for hours, agonizing over the crucial decision of what to wear. Finally, and with some apprehension, I selected a lace-trimmed camisole I usually wore beneath blazers or low-cut blouses. The tightest jeans I owned and a pair of high-heeled ankle boots completed the outfit. I wasn't going to win any awards for style, but it was the best I could do with what I owned. "I'm wearing *underwear* as outerwear. I hope you're happy."

"I am. You made a great effort."

He took me by the hand and led me up a flight of stairs. On the upper level, music blared and multicolored lights flashed across the walls and ceiling in erratic patterns. The place was packed, and we squeezed through the crowd to get to the bar.

"Nick! Hey! How've you been?" The bartender leaned over and shouted above the loud music. "What can I get for you?"

"Just a club soda. Thanks." Nick craned his neck to look around the room. "Any of my…friends around tonight?"

He tapped his chin. "Carl was here earlier, but left about an hour ago. He said he'd be back after picking something up across town."

"Tell him to find me if you see him before I do."

"Will do." He turned to me. "And what can I get you, miss?"

I shook my head. "I'm good for now."

"Are you sure?" Nick asked. "It's on me."

"No, thanks. I'm fine."

He bent down, bringing his face nearer to

mine so he didn't have to yell. "Still not letting your guard down around me yet?"

I didn't pull away. "I willingly got into your car and let you drive. What more do you want?"

"True, true." His deep voice reverberated through me, sending tingles over my skin. "It's probably best we're both alert, anyway."

He offered me his glass of club soda, and I took a sip. The club was much warmer than the streets outside, and my perception of the higher temperature wasn't helped by knowing Nick was paying close attention to my every move. "We might have some time to kill," he said, inching closer to me. "Do you want to dance?"

I burst out laughing, loud enough to attract the attention of some nearby patrons. "I don't dance."

He drew back so I could see his wide smile. "Everybody can dance."

"Not *well*." I shook my head. "No way."

Nick glanced around the room again. "Plenty of men noticed you when we walked in, Celeste. I bet they're still watching you." He ducked down to whisper into my ear. "Unless you go out there with me, you'll be fending off advances from potentially dangerous strangers for the rest of the night. So, what do you say?"

Though I rolled my eyes at his mockery of my concerns, I felt my cheeks burning regardless. "Well, if it's you or them..." I said, trying to keep my tone light. I gulped down the rest of the club soda and set the glass back on the bar. "How do I keep letting myself get into these situations with you?"

"Hey, I'm not forcing you to do anything. I never have."

I tried to get away with standing at the very edge of the dance floor. Nick dragged me further into the crowd. "Come on!" he shouted. "This'll be fun!"

Someone bumped into me and I almost lost my balance. "If you say so."

I stayed in one place and swung my arms a little bit, attempting to avoid the erratic flailing of the people around me. Nick bounced in front of me in time with the beat. "That's it?"

he prodded.

Sighing, I tried to shuffle from side to side without colliding with anyone. He laughed and shook his head. "You're really terrible at this."

"I told you."

"All you have to do is move to the music." He took my hands. "Feel the rhythm flow through you and just let yourself go."

"You sound like an idiot." I went limp, letting him maneuver my arms. "And this is a shortcoming I can live with."

Nick spun one of my arms over my head, turning me around. He let go of my hand, only to pull me back against him. "I refuse to believe there's something you can't do."

His hands slid down my sides, coming to rest on either side of my hips. Unsure of what to do with my own hands, I rested them on top of his, feeling the warmth of his skin. Every time he moved, I moved with him, his firm grip guiding me. "Bend your knees a little," he instructed. "You don't have to stand like you're in a courtroom."

I did as I was told, rubbing against his body

in the process. His hot breath fanned across my bare shoulder, and one arm snaked around my waist as we swayed together. The music and the lights swirled together in an intoxicating blur, although I'd only had the club soda to drink. I closed my eyes and leaned back against his shoulder, trying to take his advice and lose myself to the rhythm he set.

"Nick! I heard you were looking for me."

He straightened, releasing me. I turned around to find the source of the interruption. "Hey, Carl," Nick greeted the older, heavyset man behind us.

Carl jerked his head to the side and started walking off the dance floor. Nick grabbed my hand and followed after him. We headed toward a secluded booth in the back corner of the room; I didn't question why it was the only empty one in the row. The music wasn't as loud here and we didn't have to scream to be heard. Nick and I slid across the cushions on one side, and our companion sat opposite us.

"Nicky, Nicky, Nicky." Carl sighed and tapped his thick fingers together. "I have to say,

I'm a little surprised to see you here."

"And why is that?" Nick propped his forearms on the table. "You expected me to be sitting in jail for a crime I didn't commit?"

He turned to me. "You a cop?"

"No," I said. "Do I look like one?"

"Doesn't mean anything."

Nick leaned back and grabbed the hem of his t-shirt. "Do you want to check me for a wire, Carl? Should I strip down right here for you?"

"That's not necessary." His eyes narrowed. "I just don't know what you want from me."

"Anything that can help me out."

He said nothing. Nick folded his arms over his chest. "We were friends once," he said, his voice quiet. "I thought I could count on you."

The intensity of Carl's glare didn't waver. "I'm not stupid. I don't want to end up in the same position as you're in right now."

"He'll never know—"

"Bullshit." His eyes darted from side to side. "How many people do you think will see us talking to each other before we leave?"

"Then I guess you're already fucked." Nick smirked. "Frankie will assume the worst if he hears you were talking to me, anyway, so you could at least point me in the right direction."

Silence.

"You're really going to let me rot for something Frankie did? Or at least orchestrated?" He uncrossed his arms and laid his hands flat on the table. "Come on, Carl. Give me *something*."

Carl let out a long breath. "You're right. I don't want to see you go down for this, even though it was dumb of you to think you could just walk away."

"I know, I know."

Even though no one sat or stood near us, he glanced around the vicinity again. "Frankie's got this new girlfriend. Pretty little thing. Smart, too, but that bitch is crazy." He looked at me. "Sorry."

I shrugged.

"She thought Willy shorted them after a big deal the other week," Carl went on. "I swore she was going to claw his eyes out."

"Charming." Nick raised his eyebrows. "So, she's doing his dirty work for him now?"

"She flies under the radar pretty easy, and Frankie likes that." Once again, Carl's attention veered back in my direction. "You looking for any work, sweetheart?"

Nick jumped in before I said something that would land us both in trouble. "And you think she killed Sherri?"

"I can't say for sure. And if she did, I don't know if she was following Frankie's explicit instructions, or if he just planted the seeds in her head." He shook his head. "Women. They'll either stand by you in the name of love until the end of the world, or they'll fuck you over to save themselves at the first opportunity. Frankie's girl could go either way, and that's all I'm telling you tonight."

"It's a start. Thank you." Nick nudged me and I stood up, with him close behind. "Stay safe, Carl. I really hope me being here doesn't cause you any trouble."

"Yeah, me too." He nodded at me and winked. "It was nice meeting your friend."

I offered him a tight-lipped smile.

Nick ushered me around the edge of the dance floor to the staircase. "Sorry about Carl," he said. "He's a little...uh...jaded."

"Eh, I've heard worse." I looked at him as we walked down the steps, trying to hide my amusement. "At least I learned there's some reasoning behind why I agreed to your schemes in the first place."

"Oh? What's that?"

"Bitches are crazy."

Nick laughed and gave my shoulder a squeeze. "You were a good sport tonight."

"I'm glad you thought so," I said. "But that's not the important part. Did you get everything?"

He pulled his cell phone out of his pocket. "It was recording the whole time. Good thing he didn't call my bluff and check me." After tapping the screen a few times, he put the phone away. "The quality's probably crappy, but I got most of the conversation. And thanks for the brief education on New York's one-party consent law."

"That's what I'm here for, right? Fingers crossed we don't wind up needing to use it, as I'd have a *lot* of explaining to do." I tried not to cringe at a variety of hypothetical scenarios, ranging from some awkward conversations at work to the end of my career.

We retrieved our belongings from the coat check and went outside to brave the cold. The entire drive out of the city was spent arguing over whether to turn what we'd learned over to the police yet. Instead of getting into my own car in the parking lot at Meadowbrook Gardens, I followed Nick back into his apartment without thinking about it. "I still think we need some outside help," I said. "You and I can only get so far on our own."

"We did pretty well tonight, didn't we?" He took off his jacket and flung it onto the armchair before sitting on the couch. "But we don't have to make a decision right this second. It is getting late, after all."

"Late?" I laughed. "It's after two o'clock in the morning. I can't even tell you the last time I saw this hour."

He smiled, peering at me through the hair that had flopped into his eyes. "I guess I should let you go, then."

"I'll talk to you soon."

My hand was on the doorknob when he called out to me. "You know, you don't have to leave if you don't want to."

I froze, afraid to turn around and meet his gaze. Behind me, I heard him get up and cross the room. "It's completely up to you."

Nick leaned against the wall next to me, but I refused to look at him. "Why do you do this to me?" I muttered, more to myself than him.

"I'm not doing anything."

Open the door, leave, go home, stay out of trouble.... The voices in my head kept telling me what a bad idea it would be to get further involved with this man. I ignored them and turned to the side. Piercing hazel eyes bored into me, and I tried not to tremble beneath their magnetic power.

"You know what I like about you, Celeste?" he said, shattering the growing silence.

I swallowed. "What?"

He towered over me, close enough to touch. "You keep me on my toes. I never know what I'm going to get with you." His thumb and forefinger rubbed the lapel of my coat. "There's the strait-laced attorney in her respectable suits. Then there's the casual, curious woman who first showed up at my apartment."

Gently, he pushed the coat off my shoulders. With one finger, he traced a line over the flimsy strap of my camisole. "And then somewhere deep inside, there's a bad girl hiding, waiting to come out."

The light touch on my skin drove me wild, and I tilted my face upward. Our instant attraction to each other had been simmering for weeks, and I was ready for it to be unleashed. The decision had been made. "I want to be your bad girl tonight," I whispered.

Nick's hand slid from my shoulder up my neck. Threading his fingers through my hair, he kissed me, his lips soft, yet firm. I leaned into his chest and opened my mouth for him. His tongue mingled with mine as he held me in place.

Beneath my palms, I felt his breathing quicken. Our explorations became more daring, and I nipped at his bottom lip. His fist tightened in my hair and he backed me against the door. "Celeste," he murmured. "I have to ask...."

"Mm?"

He stopped kissing me, but didn't pull away. "Do you still think I killed Sherri?"

I was caught off-guard by the question, my mind spinning from the sudden change of topic. "No," I finally got out.

Nick straightened and stared down at me. "You hesitated."

My pulse raced even faster. "I didn't...I mean—"

"It's fine. I know the truth." His fingers returned to the strap of the camisole, but this time, they skated along the edge of the lace trim encasing my breasts. "And who knows? Maybe you get a little thrill out of not knowing for sure. Maybe you like the risk, the danger."

I didn't have a good answer for him. All I

could do was quiver at his feathery touch as I remained enthralled by his intense gaze. "But know this," Nick went on. "I saw the crime scene photographs. Whoever did that to Sherri was enraged, out of control. And I...." He reached between us and seized my wrists with surprising force. "I'm always in control."

He pinned my hands over my head, slamming them against the door with a resounding thud. His mouth reclaimed mine, his tongue plunging inside. I squirmed, testing the strength of his grip. He had me trapped; the more I struggled, the more aroused I became.

His body pressed forward, further immobilizing me. My hips rolled to meet the massive bulge in his pants. A light moan escaped my lips and my panties grew damp as I tried to feel more of his cock.

Without releasing me, he stood between my legs. I should have been exhausted, but I was awake, *alive*. All my senses went into overdrive. I felt the solid door digging into my back, matched by the outline of his erection on the other side of me. I tasted the sweet velvet of his tongue tangling with mine. My heartbeat pulsed in my ears and I swore I could hear the fire streaking through my veins. Everything about him excited me, and I craved more.

Nick brought one of my arms down while holding the other in place. He directed my hand to his cock, and I groped its thickness through his jeans. "See what you do to me?" he said, his voice little more than a growl. "You've been tempting me all night. I could take you right here."

All I could think about was getting him inside me, satisfying that burning hunger. "So do it," I breathed.

He laughed, a wicked laugh that sent another shiver down my spine. "Impatient, are we?" His free hand snaked beneath my shirt and skimmed around to my back. He abruptly yanked me from the door, holding me tight so I didn't stumble. Once I regained my balance, he grabbed the hem of the camisole and pulled it up.

Our lips collided in another crushing kiss

before the silky garment even hit the floor. He attacked my bra next, and I didn't know whether he took the time to unfasten the clasps or tore it off. His palms roamed over my skin, rising to cup my breasts. He kneaded and massaged, teasing at the hardened nipples, and I moaned into his mouth.

Desperate to feel more of him against me, I fumbled with the bottom of his shirt. He jerked away and shook his head. "Uh-uh," he said. Though he smiled, something savage gleamed in his eyes. "Not until I say so."

Nick nudged me backward until my thighs hit the arm of the sofa. "Turn around," he ordered.

I did as he said. His palms returned to my body, exploring, caressing, fondling. He brushed my hair aside to kiss my neck. As he left a trail of light nibbles, his fingers unbuttoned my jeans. One hand slipped inside, stroking me through a thin layer of wet satin.

My hips sought out more of him, but he withdrew. His tormenting chuckle echoed in my ears, and he reached for the waistband of my jeans. Slowly, he pushed them down, kissing a line down the back of one of my legs as he tugged them to my ankles. My panties followed suit, leaving me exposed and trembling with anticipation.

Nick stood again and brought his lips back to my ear. "Bend over," he said. "Let me get a good look at that sweet pussy of yours."

Flames ignited in my cheeks and spread throughout me like an inferno. Somehow, I found his demands impossible to resist. I leaned forward on the sofa, turning my head to the side and resting my forearms on one of the cushions. My legs shook as he pushed them as far apart as they would go while still linked by my pants. A single finger skated along the edge of my pussy, and I gasped.

He held me steady with one hand on my back while he pressed inside me. A second finger joined the first, gliding in and out in an easy rhythm. I grasped the fabric of the cushion and tried to meet his pace, but every time I pushed back, his fingers stilled. When I stopped moving along with him, he resumed his deepening thrusts. I had no choice but to play by the rules he set.

Pleasure constricted in my muscles and I panted for air. I closed my eyes and waited for relief. Just when I thought I would tumble into bliss, his hands vanished from my body and he stepped away. "Nick!" I gasped, my breaths ragged. "Please...I need to...."

"Oh, you will. I promise." He gave my ass a playful squeeze, letting his hand linger. "I'll be right back. And while I'm gone...." Fingertips dug into my flesh. "*Do not move.*"

I lay there, sprawled across the couch, and watched him leave the room. In his absence, the room's chilly air hit my slickened pussy. My legs ached from being spread in that awkward position for so long, and lust clouded my mind. I needed to be filled, to have my carnal appetite sated, yet I stayed there in my precarious state, waiting for him.

Nick emerged from the bedroom holding a wrapped condom. "Oh, Celeste, you are a treat." The predatory grin made its appearance again. "I half-expected you to finish yourself off, but I'm glad you listened to me. I'm sure you'll agree it's better this way."

He stood by the sofa, just far enough away so I couldn't reach him if I dared try. His shirt joined mine on the floor, giving me my first glimpse of the lean muscles of his chest. I didn't have long to admire them, though, as the scratch of his zipper caught my attention. At long last, his cock was freed, jutting upward as he finished removing his pants. I swallowed while I stared, fantasizing about its full length buried deep inside me.

The wrapper crinkled as he opened it, and he took his place between my legs. He ran his finger over my dampened cleft again and I whimpered. "You've been so good tonight," he said. "Or bad. Whichever you prefer." He caressed the swell of my hips. "Now, let's have some real fun."

With one swift motion, he impaled my cunt. I cried out and braced myself for the next onslaught. Over and over he pumped into me, forging deeper with each thrust. The pressure of his cock seared across my nerves, and my clit rubbed against the edge of the couch as he dominated me. This time, I knew there'd be no stopping either of us.

The room blurred in front of me, and I closed my eyes. I buried my face in the cushion and let him ride me hard. Every inch of me tingled with the expectation of release, from the ends of my fingers down to the tips of my toes. Even my hair felt like it was about to catch fire. All I could do was hang on for the ride.

Nick's breathing grew strained and his grip on me tightened. His relentless assault on my pussy never wavered. With a primal grunt, he slammed into me so hard, the couch gouged the wooden floorboards. The last explosion of energy kindled my own orgasm, and I screamed into the cushion. Pulse after pulse of ecstasy shot through my core, making me writhe uncontrollably. All the air whisked from my lungs and I lost myself to the euphoric haze.

My body hung over the side of the sofa like a rag doll. Once Nick was out of the way, I used my last bit of strength to kick off my shoes and jeans. He sat beside me on the couch and pulled me close to him. Our limbs entwined in a sweaty tangle as I caught my breath.

"I'm glad you decided to stay," he said, giving my hair a teasing tug.

"Me too." I rested my head on his shoulder and gazed up at him. "I think we both got what we needed tonight."

***

By the time spring rolled around, the DA's office had dropped all charges against Nick Lattimer. More evidence had surfaced, evidence I persuaded him to bring to the police. Colin hadn't been completely convinced of his innocence, but he didn't think he could win over a jury with the available facts.

I'd managed to downplay my involvement in Nick's amateur investigation. I don't think anyone in the office ever realized the extent of the assistance I'd offered, yet even after the charges were dismissed, I felt uncomfortable at work. Though I'd been thrilled with the opportunity to work there when I was first hired, I no longer believed I was in the right place to further develop my love of the law.

A well-known criminal defense firm took more interest in my role in Nick's case than the DA's office had when I applied for a new job. After deciding the quiet suburbs weren't for me, I accepted the job in Manhattan and immersed myself in city life. The heart of New York wasn't always as glamorous as movies and TV made it out to be, but in my heart, I knew it was the right choice.

I wasn't the only one to move down to the city. Even though his name had been cleared, Nick wasn't comfortable staying in his apartment at Meadowbrook Gardens. I expressed concerns for his safety, but he assured me he had no intentions of returning to his previous life and swore it would be easier to keep a low profile in a city of millions.

We agreed to keep our relationship casual. He was still trying to figure out what his next step should be while I embarked on an adventurous new career path. Despite our differences, we made time to get together on a semi-regular basis. He served as a reminder to let loose every now and then and enjoy life outside of work. After the first night we shared, I had no desire to say good-bye and forget about him.

Some people disparaged the work my colleagues and I performed, claiming we were finding ways for violent criminals to go free. I, however, had learned firsthand how there are two sides to every story. In my role as a defense attorney, I felt an obligation to pursue the truth, no matter how a case originally appeared. All of this had started with Nick, who had been wrongfully accused of murder.

At least I was fairly certain I wasn't sleeping with a killer....

---------------▼---------------

About the Author

Thea Landen lives in New York with her husband and children. Though she's dabbled in all romantic subgenres, she has a special love for sci-fi, fantasy, and adventure... anything that pushes the imagination beyond its usual limits. When she's not writing, she's either knitting or crocheting, playing video games, or pretending to enjoy cardio and squats.

www.thealanden.com

Andromeda's Tear

Subscribe to Thea's newsletter for your free e-copy of Andromeda's Tear at http://eepurl.com/ha7JzT or www.thealanden.com!

Sienna seems to have it all: a lavish home on an upscale space station, a lucrative job waiting for her at her father's company, and a wealthy bachelor chasing after her. Just because she has an enviable life, however, doesn't mean she's satisfied with her place in the universe. When she meets Ace, a teleporter repairman by day and enterprising criminal by night, she spots an opportunity to make some much-needed changes and quench her desire for excitement. Together, they plot to steal a priceless sapphire from the man Sienna's parents want her to marry. Will their interplanetary jewel heist succeed, or will their attraction to each other get in the way?

Train Hard, Rest Harder
Available Now!

Between her fast-paced career and managing her household for her family, Julia is always on the go. Her busy schedule leaves little time for her to pursue her own interests and hobbies, save for one activity: the gym she attends with her husband, Rob. The high-intensity classes they take allow her to destress, yet, as with every other aspect of her life, she constantly pushes herself to achieve her fitness goals.

Afraid his wife is at risk of burning out, Rob conspires with Tristan, one of the trainers at the gym, and forms a plan in order to encourage Julia to take a break from all her obligations. They present her with their scheme, informing her how she and Tristan will be staying at his family's secluded lake house for a long weekend, during which she is under strict orders not to cook, clean, or answer any messages from work. As she processes everything they've plotted behind her back, Rob privately tells her he's noticed her attraction to their trainer. To her surprise, he grants her permission to do anything she wants with Tristan during their weekend together...*anything*.

They embark on their trip, and Julia wonders if she'll be able to disconnect from her responsibilities and relax for a few days. She also contemplates whether she can be intimate with another man, despite Rob's reassurances. Will this weekend with her trainer fulfill all her fantasies?

***

Sitting up on the bench, I sipped from the water bottle, drinking it more slowly than I had after finishing my run. "Some lower body and we're done," Tristan said. "I won't torture you with too much core work today. You know, since you're supposed to be taking it easy this weekend and everything."

I pursed my lips. "Thanks ever so much."

Once I stood, I let him coach me through weighted lunges in all directions and a few rounds of deadlifts. "Almost done." His gaze flicked back and forth between me and the stack of weights. "Sorry there's no squat rack here, but I think, as we established last night, we need to make sure you're keeping up with your squats."

His words, combined with the memory of his hands on my body, increased the heat simmering inside me. "I'll make do with what we have. Front squats or goblet squats?"

"I'll let you choose."

I bent down to retrieve the dumbbells I'd used for the lunges. "Uh-uh. Try again," he said from behind me.

"What?"

"We both know you can go heavier than that."

I glanced back at him over my shoulder. "Yeah, but it's different without the rack. I have to be able to actually pick these up."

Tristan inched closer and rested one hand at the small of my back. "I know how strong you are." His breath fanned across my neck as he spoke. "Give me ten good squats and we'll call it a day."

He let his hand drop and gave my ass a quick squeeze before stepping away. I didn't realize how much I craved more of his touch until he let go of me, but there was only one way to earn it. I went to the rack against the wall and returned with the heaviest weights I thought I could get up to my chest. Blowing out a puff of air, I hoisted them into position and steadied myself for the first squat.

"Slow and controlled," he said. "And get nice and low with good form, or else I'm going to make you start from the beginning."

My legs already ached from the run

followed by the lunges, but I kept my knees pressed out to the sides as I dipped down and back up. *One*, I counted to myself. I repeated the movement, fighting to keep the tremble out of my arms as I held the dumbbells up in front of me.

"Almost there." His raspy whisper sent a different kind of shiver through my tensed muscles. "You got this."

How the weights didn't slip out of my hands, I had no idea. I maintained my grip and sank down into my heels yet again. Every time I rose presented more of a struggle, but I was determined to complete the set. Once I finished the tenth squat, I exhaled a long sigh of relief and set the dumbbells down.

Tristan was on me in a flash. He grabbed me by the waist and yanked me backward, sending me crashing into his bare chest. "I love watching you move," he growled in my ear. "Your powerful body, your flawless form...do you know how long I've been dreaming of a moment like this?"

He drew my earlobe into his mouth, giving it a

sharp nip. His palms roamed over my stomach and hips, grazing the lower edge of my bra with every stroke. When he pulled me closer, his rock-hard erection pressed alongside my ass. Dizzy with desire, I closed my eyes and leaned back, resting my head against his shoulder.

Manufactured by Amazon.ca
Acheson, AB